The Catnap Before Christmas

A Whales and Tails Mystery

by

Kathi Daley

Whales and Tails

Romeow and Juliet
The Mad Catter
Grimm's Furry Tail
Much Ado About Felines
The Legend of Tabby Hollow
The Cat of Christmas Past
The Tail of Two Tabbies
The Great Catsby
Count Catula
The Cat of Christmas Present
A Winters Tail
Taming of the Tabby
Frankencat
The Cat of Christmas Future
Farewell to Felines
The Catsgiving Feast
A Whale of a Tail
The Catnap Before Christmas

Chapter 1

Wednesday, December 11

"I think she's dead," he said.

"She's not dead," she replied.

"She sure looks dead," he argued.

"Miss Cait? Are you alive, Miss Cait?" she asked, concern present in her voice.

Go away, I thought to myself as I resisted the voices that pulled me out of the best sleep I'd had in weeks.

"You'd better dial 9-1-1," he suggested.

I opened my eyes to the orange, red, and green lights twinkling overhead. "I'm not dead, and you don't need to call 9-1-1," I assured Anastasia Walker, Archie Cunningham, and the group of choir members who knelt on the floor next to me. "I was just taking a nap."

"Why were you taking a nap under the tree?" six-year-old Anastasia asked.

Why had I been taking a nap under the tree? I tried to remember, but I wasn't completely awake, and my memory was fuzzy.

"And why were you taking a nap with a cat?" eight-year-old Archie added.

A cat? I frowned and turned my head to the side. I had been sleeping with a cat. A gorgeous, longhaired, black-and-white cat that I was certain I'd never seen before. I closed my eyes once again and tried to remember exactly how I'd gotten here.

"Are you sick?" Anastasia asked, her bright blue eyes filled with genuine concern as she brushed my hair from my face.

"No." I yawned and slowly sat up. "I'm not sick. I'm just tired." I picked up the cat and cuddled him in my arms. "Very, very, tired," I added in a soft voice.

"Are you sure?" Archie asked. "Grown-ups don't take naps unless they're sick."

"I'm sure." I forced my legs under my body and stood up.

"If you aren't sick, why did you take a nap?" Anastasia asked.

Apparently, the adorable little imp wasn't going to leave this alone. "The baby has been keeping me awake at night, and I guess it all just caught up with me." I looked at the cat, who I still cradled in my arms. Where had he come from? I glanced out the window at the dark sky. How long had I been here?

"You have a baby?" Anastasia asked, confusion evident in her eyes.

"No, I don't have a baby," I answered. "Cody and I are babysitting his cousin's baby, and I guess he's missed his mommy since he's been here and hasn't been sleeping well."

My husband, Cody West, had taken the baby to Seattle to spend the day with his aunt, who was going to be in the area on a business trip. His mother and father were both in the military and currently overseas, so Cody and I were babysitting the infant until his father returned to the States in January. Cody had invited me to go with him on the overnight trip, but I realized that his taking the baby to Seattle was actually a gift, as it afforded me an unselfish reason to spend thirty-six hours on my own. Not that I didn't love my husband and the baby whose care we'd been entrusted with, but the timing of the whole thing could have been better. Not only did we have a Christmas pageant to prepare for, but Cody and I were in the middle of a move from my little cabin to the mansion next door.

"Where's Leo?" I asked after taking a quick mental inventory of who was there and who was still missing. There were actually quite a few kids missing this evening, but having Mary and Joseph was critical if we were going to run through everyone's lines.

"What's the baby's name?" Anastasia asked, completely ignoring my question regarding the whereabouts of our Joseph.

"Sammy."

"Is he cute?" Anastasia asked.

I paused and looked at the six-year-old, who seemed to be a lot more fascinated with the idea of my having a baby than she was with rehearsing the play. She was going to make an adorable angel with all those long blond ringlets. "He is cute. Have you seen Leo? We really need to get started if we are going to get anything done."

"I guess his dad couldn't bring him on account of the fire," Denise Partridge said.

"Fire?" Leo's dad was a firefighter, and he was a single dad. I supposed if there had been a fire, he might be tied up and unable to ferry his son to rehearsal.

"The fire at the Santa House," Denise specified.

My brow shot up. "The Santa House is on fire?"

"It *was* on fire." Denise narrowed her gaze. "How long have you been sleeping?"

Good question. I remembered stopping off at the church on my way into town to take care of a whole slew of errands. I wanted to drop off the costumes my Aunt Maggie had made for the play but had shipped to the house my older sister Siobhan and her husband Finn now lived in with their son, Connor. Normally, on Wednesdays I worked at Coffee Cat Books, the bookstore I owned with my best friend, Tara O'Brian, but with Cody and Sammy out of town, I'd taken the day off to get some things that had been piling up taken care of.

"Miss Cait, are you okay?" Anastasia asked yet again.

I took a deep breath and chased the last of the sleep from my brain. "I'm fine." I looked at Denise. "You said the Santa House was on fire?"

"It was, but I think they must have it out by now," Mitch Brown, one of my ten-year-olds responded. Mitch was the narrator for the play and the oldest member of the cast.

"Was anyone hurt?" I asked.

"My dad told my mom that Santa was dead," Mitch answered.

"Santa's dead?" Anastasia began to cry.

I looked down at the cat in my arms. Santa was dead! A cat had shown up! Suddenly everything felt a lot more serious. "We're going to take a short break," I announced.

"Break?" Seven-year-old Dennis White asked. "We just got here."

"I know, but I need to make a phone call. It's important. While I'm making my call, you can set up the stage for the manger scene. I won't be long." I set the cat down on the floor to the delight of the kids and stepped into the hallway. Leaving the door open so I could keep an eye on my cast of actors aged six to ten, I dialed Cody's number.

"Come on, answer," I said aloud as the call went straight through to voice mail.

Cody was going to be in Seattle until tomorrow and was most likely visiting with Sammy's aunt, so I guess I shouldn't be surprised that he hadn't picked up. I did notice two missed calls from Tara, as well as a missed call from Siobhan. I called Siobhan back first.

"Cait. Good. Where are you?"

"At the church. I just heard about the Santa House. What happened?"

"I'm not sure exactly."

I could hear sirens and noise in the background, so I had to assume Siobhan was still in town. She was, after all, the mayor, so it made sense she would head to the scene.

Siobhan continued. "I was just getting ready to head home for the day when Finn called to tell me the Santa House was on fire. My first thought was for all the kids who could have been injured, but then I realized the house didn't open until five on weekdays and it was only four. I called Cassie and asked her to pick Connor up from day care, and then I headed into town. It's bad. Really bad. It looks like Tom Miller is dead, although no one has been able to get inside to confirm that. The Santa House is a total loss."

"I've got a choir room full of kids, or I'd come down to help out," I said. "Was anyone else injured?"

"I don't know for sure. I don't think so, but the building went up fast. A few spectators had begun to gather in the area of the Santa Village and Santa House, and several people saw Tom go inside, but the fire was too hot to search the place to confirm his death or to see if there were any other victims yet. Is Cody still in Seattle?"

"Until tomorrow." I glanced at Timmy and James, who were having a sword fight with the shepherds' staffs. "I should get back to the kids. I'll call you back when I get the chance."

"I'll probably head home soon. Connor has been teething and is extra fussy, and I don't want Cassie to have to deal with the bedtime drama. I'm sure Finn is going to be a while, so just come by the house when you are done at the church."

By the time I returned to the room, the kids were totally wound up. I decided to switch things up and practice the songs for the event rather than running through everyone's lines. It was less than two weeks until the pageant, so I supposed we'd need to have some extra rehearsals before the big day. The cat who had been sleeping with me had crawled back under the tree and gone back to sleep. I supposed I should call Tansy, the witch who seemed to be the keeper of the island's magical cats. In the past, when a cat showed up accompanied by a death or disaster, it was an indicator that the animal and I had a destiny to fulfill, and that destiny usually involved helping Finn bring in the bad guy and ensure that justice was served.

"Miss Tara," the kids yelled, running toward the door that led into the auditorium. Tara taught the Sunday school classes for kids aged five to twelve, so most of the choir members knew her.

"Did you just come from town?" I asked after she took off her coat and hung it on a peg.

"Yes. The traffic was a bear." She looked at her watch. "It took me over an hour to get here."

Usually, the drive from the wharf, where Coffee Cat Books was located, to Saint Patrick's Catholic Church was less than twenty minutes. No wonder so many kids were absent tonight.

"Have you heard about the fire?"

She nodded. "Cassie was at the bookstore when Siobhan called."

Cassie was my other sister, the youngest of the five Hart siblings. She worked at the bookstore Tara and I owned now that she'd moved back to Madrona Island full-time.

"I spoke to Siobhan. She said it's bad. She thinks Tom Miller is dead."

Tara bowed her head. "I heard. I called Danny, and he filled me in. He left Aiden to hold down the bar while he went over to the Santa House to check things out."

Danny and Aiden were my brothers. They'd recently purchased and refurbished O'Malley's Bar and Grill, one of the oldest bars on the island. Since then, it seemed all the Hart siblings had spent quite a bit of time hanging out there.

"Danny said that he spoke to one of the firefighters, who told him it looked like someone set the structure on fire intentionally," Tara informed me. "Apparently, the speed with which the building was enflamed could only have been accomplished with an accelerant."

I glanced at the kids, who were all looking at us by this point. "The parents will be here to pick up the kids in thirty minutes. Why don't you hang out and we'll figure out our next move once everyone has gone?"

Tara nodded and headed to the piano. She began to belt out a tune that had all the kids singing. Cody and I usually had a pianist for choir practice, but tonight I'd planned to run lines rather than practice our songs, so I hadn't asked her to come in.

By the time I got the kids delivered to their parents, it was after eight. Tara and I decided to head over to O'Malley's to check in with the brothers after we took the cat back to the cabin and got him settled along with my dog, Max. As we pulled up to the cabin, Siobhan walked out of the main house to greet us.

"Did you get Connor to sleep?" I asked.

"I did."

"Is Finn back?"

"Not yet. I was waiting for you to get home. I thought I'd come over and we could try to make some sense of this."

I glanced at the house. "What about Connor?"

"Michael and Maggie showed up out of the blue. Marley's birthday is Friday, so they wanted to do something with her this weekend." Maggie Hart Kilian was our aunt, and she'd owned the house

Siobhan and her family lived in before gifting it to her oldest niece. While the house was now owned by the Finnegans, Maggie and her husband, Michael, had their own bedroom in it and often spent time here when they were on the island. Marley Donnelly was Maggie's best friend and ex-business partner. "Anyway, they said they'd listen for him should he wake before I get back. They are planning to go to bed early, but there's a baby monitor in their room."

"Tara and I were going to head over to the bar after we get the cat settled. You can come with us if you'd like."

"Cat?" Siobhan asked.

I opened my back door and picked up the cat.

"He's beautiful. Is he a Tansy cat?"

"I think so. He showed up at the church today. It's too late to ask Tansy about him now, but I'll ask her in the morning."

"I'd like to go with you to the bar. Let me just tell Maggie what I'm doing and grab my purse. I'll ride along with you. I think Cassie was heading over there when she left here, so maybe among all of us, we can figure out what in the heck is going on."

When we arrived at O'Malley's, we found Cassie sitting on a barstool chatting with Danny. We motioned to them that we were going to grab a table. Both Cassie and Danny joined us.

"Any news?" I asked, sliding toward the center of the booth.

"It has been confirmed that Tom Miller was inside the Santa House when it burned down," Danny said, pulling a chair up to the end of the booth.

"It was a small building. It seems like he would have had time to get out," Tara said, waving for Aiden to bring us a bottle of wine.

"It seems the fire was started by a small explosion," Danny informed us. "It's too early to know much, but it looked as if Tom might have suffered a blow to the head. Like I said, nothing is known for certain yet, but I heard one of the firefighters say that it appeared that Tom might have been unconscious before the flames got to him."

"Poor Tom," I said. "I guess his daughter must have been notified."

"I guess," Danny responded.

Tom was a widower with one child, an adult daughter who lived in Chicago. On the outside, he seemed to have lived a lonely life since his wife died, but I knew he volunteered in the community and seemed to keep busy. I was really going to miss him.

"Everyone want a glass?" Aiden asked, setting a bottle of the wine he knew I preferred on the table.

Tara, Cassie, and I confirmed that we did, but Siobhan asked Aiden to bring her a diet cola instead.

"I just don't understand who would blow up the Santa House," Cassie said after Aiden left to fetch the glasses and Siobhan's soda.

"I've been thinking about that," Siobhan said. "I can't help but wonder if the Santa House was the intended victim or if it was Tom."

I wrinkled my nose. "What do you mean? Why would anyone intentionally kill Tom Miller?"

"Why would anyone intentionally burn down the Santa House?" Siobhan countered.

I supposed that she had a point.

"Tom worked the Santa House Monday through Fridays from five to nine," Tara joined in. "If he was the target, the arsonist would have been able to anticipate where he'd be when the explosion occurred."

"He was there an hour early," I countered. "Did he always show up an hour early?"

No one seemed to know.

"Setting an explosion to go off at four when the house opens at five makes sense from the standpoint of minimizing human casualties, but why kill Tom in that manner?" Danny asked. "If he was the target, why not just kill him in his home? He does live alone. It would have been a lot less messy to simply wait for him to be home alone and then take care of things at that time."

I paused to consider the situation. "We need to find out if it was Tom's habit to show up so early. If not, if he usually didn't show up at the house until closer to five, then maybe the person who set off the explosion didn't intend there to be any deaths at all."

"Then why blow up the house?" Cassie asked.

"Not everyone likes Santa or Christmas," I reminded the group.

"So maybe we are just looking for a Grinch who wanted to destroy part of the town's Christmas celebration," Tara said. "How can we find out?"

I wasn't sure, but I suspected that if there was someone out there intent on destroying Christmas, the Santa House wouldn't be the only casualty we'd see.

Chapter 2

Thursday, December 12

By the following morning, we had the answer to the question as to whether Tom or the Santa House itself had been the target of the arsonist. During the overnight hours, the big tree in the park used by the community as the island's Christmas tree had been cut down, the reindeer that had been hung to span Main Street had been shot down, and the manger scene in front of Saint Patrick's had been vandalized.

"It looks as if we have a Grinch on the loose," Tara said to me as we shelved the order of new books that had arrived.

I glanced at the Christmas Village Tara had been lovingly collecting and displaying ever since we'd opened the store. "Do you think whoever is doing this is finished, or do you think that he's only just gotten started?"

Tara bit her lower lip. "I don't know. I hope he or she or whoever is doing this is finished doing whatever they feel needs to be done."

"Let's just go with the generic 'he' for now," I suggested in an attempt to simplify things. "I know we don't know if the vandal is a he or she, but saying he or she every time feels cumbersome."

"Okay, then, I hope he is done doing whatever it is he feels he needs to do. We are lucky there haven't been more deaths. If this guy continues wreaking havoc on the town, who knows who might end up getting in his way?"

I folded my arms across my chest. "I still can't believe Tom is gone. He gave so much to this town. In my mind, Tom is the reason we even had the Santa House. He was playing the role of the jolly man in red for decades."

Tara let out a slow breath. "Yeah. What happened to Tom wasn't fair. We need to figure out who did it." She looked at my still-unnamed cat, who I'd brought into the bookstore with me today. "Have you had a chance to meet with Tansy?"

I shook my head. "She didn't answer when I called, but there was a note on the door of Herbalities letting everyone know that she and Bella were on a retreat. The note indicated they'd be back today, so I'm hoping I'll catch them either at the store or at home later."

Herbalities was the store Bella and Tansy owned together. In addition to medicinal herbs, they sold creams and lotions and offered fortune-telling services. They had never admitted to actually being witches, but based on what I'd observed over the years, there was no doubt in my mind that they were the real deal.

Tara picked up the empty box she'd been unpacking, crushed it, and headed into the backroom with it. A few minutes later, she emerged with a box of mugs, which she set out on the display table. Coffee Cat Books was best known for its coffee and specialty beverages, which could be sipped while our customers hung out with the cats in the cat lounge, but we did a pretty good business selling books and novelty items as well.

"The town is hosting a holiday craft fair this weekend, and of course the following weekend is the big Christmas on the Island event. I wonder if we should cancel at least this weekend's event until someone can get a handle on what's going on," Tara said.

"It would be up to the event committee to cancel the craft fair, and I don't see them doing that. The event is being held in the community center. That's just one building to protect. I'm sure Finn is all over getting extra security set up for the weekend."

"I guess it would be sort of hard for someone to sabotage the event now that everyone is watching for it. But the Santa House burned to the ground right there in the middle of town while dozens of people milled around."

"The small explosion that ignited the fire must have been set up on a timer," I suggested.

"Do you know that for certain?" Tara asked.

"No. I'll stop by to talk to Finn after I walk down to Herbalities to see if our resident witches have returned. Do you want me to bring us some lunch?"

"Maybe a sandwich from the Driftwood. If you do talk to Finn, you might ask him about the food vendors who have been hanging out in the park and near the ferry terminal all month. While it might be hard to sabotage the community center with all the extra security, Finn can't hire security guards to protect everyone selling hot cocoa or roasted chestnuts."

I set the small Santa House Tara had ordered for our village in the middle of the miniature town square after I'd unpacked it. My heart squeezed in protest as I thought of Tom once again. If there was a Grinch out there trying to ruin Christmas, I was going to find and stop him before anyone else got hurt.

Once Tara and I had finished unpacking the delivery we'd received that morning, I pulled on my coat, hat, and gloves and headed down the street. I hoped that Bella and Tansy would be back. I suspected the cat who'd shared my nap was a Tansy cat, but until she confirmed that or he did something simply amazing, I had no way of knowing that for certain.

When I arrived at the store, I found the door unlocked, so I let myself in. The shop looked to be empty, so I called out, "Tansy. It's Cait."

"Cait," Tansy said, gliding down the stairs from the overhead storage area. "I've been expecting you. Did Jingles find you okay?"

"I assume Jingles is the cat who shared my nap yesterday?"

She just smiled.

"I guess you've heard what's been going on during the course of the past twenty-four hours."

"Of course, dear. Come in. We'll chat for a minute before you have to leave to meet up with Jingles down at the marina."

I frowned. "I left Jingles at Coffee Cat Books."

"Where he is safely sleeping. For now."

"Do you know who killed Tom?" I asked.

"The truth is not mine to find. Trust your instincts and trust Jingles to help you navigate the twists and turns on the road toward the truth you seek."

Twists and turns. Great. Why was it that the road to truth was never just a straight shot? "Is there anything at all you can tell me about Tom's death? Anything that will help me narrow in on the person who did it?"

"I sense pain. Deep, abiding pain that is so overwhelming as to pierce the veil of reality. Find the source of that pain, and you will find the individual you are looking for."

Leave it to Tansy to be vague. "Will there be other victims? Is there something I can do to prevent others from dying?"

Tansy paused. Eventually, she spoke again. "There will be distractions along the way. Other paths that you might be tempted to choose. But these paths will only serve to take you away from the killer you seek." Tansy took me by the hand and led me to the door. "Hurry now. There is one thing you must do before your journey begins."

Before my journey began? That sounded time-consuming, and I already had so much on my plate. Not that I had a choice. If Jingles and I were destined to find Tom's killer, that was exactly what I was going to do.

I hurried back down the sidewalk toward the marina. Tansy had said that Jingles would meet me there. I guess I had to assume that she knew what she was talking about. I'd just turned the corner where the main thoroughfare lining the downtown section of Pelican Bay met the wharf when I saw the smoke. "Oh, no." I took off at a run. The marina was mostly empty at this time of the year, but there were still a few diehard fishermen who kept their boats at the dock year-round. The smoke was coming from the boat belonging to Chappy Longwood, an old, weathered fishing captain who'd worked the waters surrounding Madrona Island since before my brothers were born. Chappy'd been a regular at O'Malley's since there'd been an O'Malley's, and my brothers gave him lunch every day on the house, so I hoped he was at the bar and not on his boat.

I pulled out my cell phone and dialed Finn's number.

"Cait," Finn answered.

"Chappy's boat is on fire. I'm on my way to see if he's there. Call the fire department. Hurry."

As I ran down the wharf past Coffee Cat Books, I noticed Jingles just up ahead. I ran faster. The fire looked small at this point, so I figured if Chappy was on board, I had a good chance of getting to him before it was too late. Chappy had adopted Cosmo, one of the magical cats I'd worked with previously. I hoped he was okay as well.

When I arrived at the boat, I didn't even stop to think; I boarded and looked around. Neither Chappy nor Cosmo seemed to be on board, so I found a hose and began siphoning water from the sea to extinguish the small fire someone had set on the deck of the old boat. It didn't take long to extinguish the pile of objects someone had decided to burn. The pile included an old Christmas stocking, a wooden Santa statue, and a box of assorted tree ornaments. It wasn't a lot, but I was willing to bet it was all the ornaments Chappy had. I was also willing to bet they meant a lot to him.

I could hear sirens in the distance as I pulled out my phone and called Danny. "Are you at O'Malley's?"

"I am."

"Is Chappy there?"

"He is."

"Is Cosmo with him?"

"He is. What's with all the questions?"

"There's been another fire. It was on Chappy's boat. I got there shortly after it was ignited and managed to get it put out before it did any real damage." I looked down at the smoldering Christmas decorations. "Finn just pulled up. Don't let Chappy come back to the marina on his own. I don't want to give the guy a heart attack."

"I'll come with him. Is the boat still livable?"

"Yeah. The fire was actually confined to a small pile of his belongings. I don't think there is any damage to the boat itself. After what happened at the Santa House, Finn is going to want to take a look around to make sure there aren't any additional charges set to go off, so you might want to stall. Let Chappy finish his lunch and then tell him."

"Okay." I heard Danny blow out a breath. "If you are still on that boat, get off. Like you just said, we don't know if the fire you extinguished was the only charge that was set or if there is a much larger kaboom just waiting to happen."

Chapter 3

Chappy showed up with Danny by the time Finn had confirmed that there were no additional explosives on the boat and it was safe to board. I felt so bad for the poor guy. He didn't have much, and I knew he really cherished what he did have. Finn didn't want Chappy staying on the boat until the guys from the crime lab could go through it with a fine-tooth comb, so Aiden, who had a much larger apartment than Danny's tiny place over the bar, offered to let him and Cosmo stay with him. I really did have the best brothers! Of course, my sisters were pretty awesome as well.

"What time is Cody coming back to the island?" Danny asked after we'd all been told we were free to go.

"He's coming on the last ferry."

"Maybe we should get together later to try to figure out a strategy. I know that Finn is all over this, but you are the one with the magical cat."

Danny had a point. One of the reasons the gang tended to get involved in Finn's cases was because he didn't have any full-time help on the island, and as Danny said, I did usually have a magical cat who, if history served, would probably be the one to provide the clue we needed to figure out what had happened.

"It's gotten harder to meet now that you have the bar, Siobhan and Finn have Connor, and Cody and I have Sammy, at least temporarily," I said.

"Aiden can cover the bar. I covered lunch, and this will be a weeknight in the off-season. Maggie and Michael are at Finn and Siobhan's, so maybe they would be willing to watch Connor. We can meet at your cabin, and you can put Sammy to bed."

"I suppose that will work. As long as Maggie and Michael don't have plans. I'll check with Siobhan and call you to let you know if our plan works for them. I'll invite Tara and Cassie as well. I assume you'll bring the beer."

Danny nodded.

"Okay. I'll stop by to pick up a few pizzas, and I'll text Cody to let him know what we are doing." I thought about my cozy little cabin, where so many of the Scooby meetings had been held. I was really going to miss it once the move was complete and I turned the keys over to Cassie. When Cody asked me to marry him, I'd really wanted to, but I wasn't sure I'd been ready for all the changes that came along with the change in marital status.

After speaking to both Finn and Chappy, I picked up Jingles and headed back to the bookstore. The cat lounge was empty today because I'd found homes for every single feline entrusted to my care other than those that were truly unadoptable, so I let Jingles nap on the sofa in the otherwise empty lounge.

"I miss the cats," Tara said.

"I'm going to pick up a vanload from the kill shelter in Seattle this weekend. I was going to do it this week, but somehow it didn't work out."

"How many permanent residents do you currently have at the sanctuary?" she asked.

"Eight. They are happy and comfortable, but they are still aggressive to most humans and to other small animals, so I don't think they are ever going to be suitable for permanent homes. There was a time when we couldn't keep up with the influx of cats brought to us, but things have changed, and we actually have very few drop-offs now."

The Harthaven Cat Sanctuary had initially been the brainchild of my Aunt Maggie when she'd lived on Madrona Island. Our mayor at the time had made it his personal mission to free the island of our feral cat population, and had made it legal to get rid of the cats by any means possible, including extermination. Maggie wanted to create a space where the cats could safely and comfortably live out their lives, so she'd used her own money to build the sanctuary. Now that Mayor Bradley was gone and Siobhan was mayor, it was no longer legal to kill cats. Most of the island's residents simply let them be unless they became a real problem, so the number of cats dropped off at our doorstep had decreased dramatically.

Maggie had left the island after marrying the love of her life, so Siobhan, Cassie, and I took care of the cats. We could continue to take care of our permanent residents until they passed of natural causes and then shut the place down, but all three of us felt that what we did was important, and I did have this nifty cat lounge, which helped us place the cats entrusted to us, so when things got slow I went to the mainland and imported cats in need of rescue.

"It seems like your Christmas kitty is the lazy sort," Tara commented.

"He does seem to enjoy napping."

"I guess he feels that he deserves a nap after saving the day."

I frowned. "Maybe, although I'm not so sure he saved the day. Tansy told me about the fire. Well, that isn't exactly true, but she did point me to the marina. It occurred to me that given the fact that the cat didn't actually lead me to the fire, maybe there was another reason for him being there, so once I put the fire out and turned things over to Finn, I watched him to see what he would do."

"And...?"

"And he led me to this mistletoe. It was left on a table."

"Maybe it was Chappy's," Tara suggested.

"I asked him, and he said it wasn't. The cat was pawing at it, which makes it seem important. I have no idea why the person who set the fire on the boat would leave mistletoe behind, especially if he was expecting the boat to burn, but I can't help but wonder if that isn't exactly what he did."

"Why?"

I shrugged. "I don't know. Maybe the mistletoe is some sort of signature."

"What good is leaving a signature if it would have burned up along with the boat?"

Tara was right. Leaving something behind made no sense. Still, I had a feeling that that was exactly what the guy had done. "I wonder if anyone noticed mistletoe at the scenes of the vandalism that didn't result in complete destruction."

"I suppose you could ask Finn."

The big tree in the park had been cut down, the reindeer that had been hung to span Main Street had been shot down, and the manger scene in front of Saint Pat's had been vandalized. If the vandal had left something behind at those scenes, perhaps the item left behind had survived.

"I never did stop by to speak to him or to pick up our lunch. I'll go now. By the way, Danny and I discussed having a Scooby meeting tonight after Cody gets back. He said Aiden would handle the bar. Are you in?"

"Always."

"I'll call Siobhan to check with her, but if Maggie and Michael can watch Connor, we'll have it at the cabin. Danny is bringing beer, and I'll grab a few pizzas."

The local sheriff's office where Finn kept his desk was just a few doors down from the Driftwood Café. I figured I'd stop by to chat with him if he was back from the incident at the boat, and then grab the sandwiches. If he wasn't back in his office yet, I supposed I could wait to speak to him that evening, provided he was able to come to our sleuthing meeting, which he wasn't always able to do.

"Oh good, you're here," I said as I walked in through the front door.

"I'm actually on my way out. What's up?"

"First of all, there is a Scooby meeting tonight at my place: six o'clock, beer and pizza provided.

Second of all, did you find mistletoe at the scene of any of the vandalisms?"

Finn looked surprised. "You know, we did. Both Mary and Joseph were holding mistletoe when I responded to the vandalism of the manger at Saint Patrick's, and there was a pile of mistletoe on the stump where the Christmas tree in the park once stood."

"And the reindeer that were shot down?"

"I didn't notice mistletoe there, but I wasn't specifically looking for it. Why do you ask?"

I held up the mistletoe Jingles found on the boat. "This was on Chappy's boat. If the boat had burned, as it was supposed to, the mistletoe would have burned as well, but it didn't, so it was there to find."

"Why would whoever is doing all this leave mistletoe behind?" Finn asked.

"I don't know. It seems ritualistic. I would say that whoever is doing this wants the mistletoe found as some sort of a signature, but with both the Santa House and Chappy's boat, the person shouldn't have had any expectation that it would survive the fires."

Finn held out his hand. I handed him the mistletoe. "If there are any more crime scenes to inspect—and I hope there won't be, but I suspect there will—I'll look for mistletoe. Did you tell Siobhan about the meeting tonight?"

"Not yet, but I will. I'm hoping Maggie and Michael can watch Connor. Cody can just put Sammy to bed; hopefully, he will sleep after his big trip."

"How has it been having the baby there?" Finn asked.

"Exhausting. Frustrating. Really inconvenient."

Finn laughed. "It sounds like you are not at all ready to have one of your own."

"I'm not. Not even a little bit. Sammy is sweet, and I know why Cody volunteered to watch him while his parents were overseas but having a baby who demands all your attention all the time is tiring. If not for Cassie, who helps out a lot, and the day care Siobhan helped me arrange, I think I would have gone off the deep end long ago."

"I guess now isn't the best time for this little experiment, with the remodel and the holidays and all."

I raised a brow. "Experiment? Do you think Cody agreed to babysit Sammy as some sort of an experiment to see if we were ready to have a baby? Because I had that exact thought when he first mentioned it."

Finn actually blushed. "Uh, no. Of course not. Cody wouldn't do that."

"What do you know?" I demanded.

"I don't know anything, and even if I did, what my brother-in-law tells me in confidence will stay in confidence, the same way you'd keep you sister's secrets."

I inhaled sharply. "Okay. I get that. But I really hope that Cody isn't doing this in the hope of trying to convince me to have a baby. Because it isn't working. After the past two sleepless weeks, I honestly feel that I may never be ready for a baby."

"I didn't think I'd ever be ready either, but now that we have Connor, I can't imagine life without him."

Chapter 4

As it turned out, everything fell in line, and every member of the Scooby Gang was able to meet that evening. I hoped Sammy would sleep right through it, despite the noise generated by having six people in my little cabin, and Cody'd assured me that the little guy had had a busy two days and would most likely sleep straight through until tomorrow morning.

As promised, I'd picked up pizzas and Danny had brought beer. Cassie had stopped to pick up sodas for those not wanting the beer, and Tara had brought dessert. Finn and Siobhan showed up with the whiteboard, as well as Finn's laptop, which I was certain held his notes to date.

"So what do we know?" I asked, once we'd all eaten and gathered around the whiteboard, which, as she always had in the past, Siobhan managed.

"Not a lot," Finn answered. "It appears as if we have a Grinch in town who is set on destroying the island's Christmas decorations, but so far I haven't come across a single witness who will admit to having seen anything. The small explosion that set off the fire in the Santa House occurred at four o'clock in the afternoon, but we don't know when the explosive device was placed in the structure. With the exception of the fire on Chappy's boat, the other incidents we know about all occurred during the overnight hours, when it was unlikely that there was anyone out and about to see anything."

"What about the fire on Chappy's boat?" I asked. "It would have had to have been set after Chappy left to go to O'Malley's for lunch. We are looking at a fairly small window of opportunity and whoever set the fire would have had to have gotten on the boat by walking along the dock in broad daylight. I know it is the off-season and there isn't a lot of activity down at the marina, but it seems like someone might have seen something."

"I went down to the marina with the intention of speaking to whoever might have been around when the fire was set, but the place was deserted," Finn shared. "I'll stop by a couple of times during the day tomorrow to see if I can find any witnesses, but our best bet might be to find out if any of the owners of the businesses on the wharf saw anything." Finn looked at Tara.

"I didn't see a thing," she answered. "Of course, Chappy's boat isn't visible from any of the windows at Coffee Cat Books."

"Yeah, I didn't notice anything either," I added.

"If the motive for everything that has occurred is simply to destroy holiday decorations, it's going to be really hard to even come up with a list of people to interview," Finn said.

"It is true that it isn't feasible to go around town asking folks how they feel about the upcoming holiday," Siobhan agreed.

"And even if that were possible, how would you be able to judge which sort of personal tragedies might set someone off and which wouldn't," Tara said. "It seems like the person who is doing this must have suffered a great loss that he associates with Christmas, but what if it is just some guy who didn't get the toy train he asked for when he was eight?"

"While in principle I agree with Tara, and I do realize that different people will classify the events in their lives as either good or bad to differing degrees, there is one person who comes to mind," Cody said. "Two years ago I covered a house fire where a Christmas tree caught fire, burning down the house and killing two of the three residents. The only survivor was a man named Clifford Little. I remember feeling so bad for the guy, who'd lost both his wife and his adult son. I wondered at the time if the fire hadn't been even more tragic than it otherwise would have been because it occurred just a few days before Christmas."

Siobhan nodded. "If anyone has a really good reason to hate Christmas, it sounds like it is that guy."

"I know Cliff," Finn said. "I don't think he's our guy, but I will stop by to have a chat with him. It also occurred to me to speak to Wilson Tyson. His wife was killed in an auto accident two days before Christmas last year."

"I get why we are discussing the residents of the island who have a reason to hate Christmas, but a man died. I think it would be fair to say that while horrific events suffered around the holidays might cause a person to come to hate the holiday associated with it, most grieving people don't go around blowing stuff up," Tara pointed out.

"That's true," Finn agreed. "Which is why I'm not putting a whole lot of stock in the idea that we will find Tom's killer by searching for individuals who have experienced a loss. Still, it is a place to start, and at the moment it is the only idea I have, other than simply talking to folks and looking for witnesses."

"Whoever did this has to have known Chappy. They had to have been on his boat at some point; otherwise, how would they know he even had decorations to burn? His decorations were pretty modest, so how would anyone know he's set them out if they hadn't been aboard the vessel?" I asked.

"Good point," Finn said.

"What about the access to the Santa House?" Siobhan asked. "Whoever rigged the small explosion must have been inside it at some point, probably at night, when no one was around. I assume the place was locked up when no one was there."

"I did think of that," Finn said. "I found out that the door had a combination lock and that a lot of people had the combination, including the entire Christmas committee, all the Santa House volunteers, the company who cleaned it, and probably a few others. And with a combination lock, it is easy to share, so we can't even limit the pool to those individuals who had a reason to have access."

"I guess because everything burned up there aren't any fingerprints to check," Tara said. "But what about fingerprints on the nativity scene in front of the church or on Chappy's decorations?"

"There were a lot of fingerprints on the nativity scene. A lot of people have handled the thing. As for Chappy's decorations, I'll check with the crime scene guys in the morning. I doubt they found anything that will help us, but I'll ask them."

I watched as Jingles walked across the room, jumped onto the sofa, and curled up in Tara's lap. He rubbed his head against her stomach, and she began to stroke his back. The two had spent more time together today than I had. I had a feeling that perhaps Tara and Jingles had bonded. I wasn't sure how happy Tara's cat, Bandit, would be when she returned home smelling of another cat, though with all the cats we had at the bookstore, I realized he must be used to it.

"Have you considered the fact that the person who killed Tom is not some sort of a Grinch but is simply using the Christmas decorations as a decoy?" I asked, remembering Tansy's warning against distractions.

"Actually, that did occur to me," Finn answered. "The first thing that happened was the burning of the Santa House. Now, while it might be true that someone who hated Christmas was motivated to burn it down, it is also possible that someone wanted Tom dead and placed the explosives in the house as a way to kill him. It might have occurred to this person that if they vandalized decorations, we'd focus on finding a suspect with a vendetta against Christmas rather than one with a motive to kill Tom."

"It does seem as if the events that took place after the Santa House burned are very minor in comparison to burning a structure to the ground with a man inside it," Danny said.

Siobhan held up her dry erase marker, poised to jot down anything relevant we might come up with.

"It seems as if we might want to generate a suspect list of individuals who might have a grudge against Tom. Right off hand, his brother-in-law comes to mind."

"Why would Tom's brother-in-law want him dead?" Cassie asked.

"Because he has been very vocal in his opinion that the death of his sister, Tom's wife, was somehow his fault," Siobhan answered.

"Didn't she die of an illness?" Cassie asked. "How could that be Tom's fault?"

"Darby thinks that Tom didn't seek out medical intervention for his wife in a timely manner and that even after he did, he didn't try hard enough to find a reason for her illness, despite the fact that her doctor assured him there was nothing more he could do."

"Let's add him to the suspect list," Finn instructed. "In fact, let's start a separate list so we can keep the individuals we feel might want to hurt Tom separate from the ones we feel might hate Christmas."

Siobhan wrote down Darby Weston's name.

"What about Gil Errington?" Cassie asked.

Gil had worked for Tom for at least a decade before Tom had to lay him off when his business ran into financial difficulties following his wife's death and his ability to manage it. Ultimately, Tom lost the business completely.

"It was a shame Tom lost his business after his wife died," I answered. "And it was very unfortunate that Gil lost his source of income as a result. But I'm not sure that Gil blamed Tom for what happened."

"Oh, he did," Cassie informed me. "Gil's daughter, Eve, is friends with Kimmy." Kimmy was one of Cassie's good friends. "The three of us hung out a few times last spring, and Eve told Kimmy that her father totally blamed Gil for what happened. According to Eve, her dad had worked hard to help Tom build his business, and devoted a decade of his own life to make sure that Miller Heating and Cooling was a success. When Tom's wife got sick, he started spending a lot of time either at home or at the hospital, and from what Eve said, her dad put in even more hours. Her dad expected that Tom would be back to work after his wife passed, but that wasn't what happened. Eve said he just let the business melt away. He stopped bidding jobs, and even the ones they did have were riddled with all sorts of problems. Eve said that by the time Tom decided to lay everyone off and close the business, her dad wasn't surprised, but he was angry that he had wasted a huge chunk of his life helping to build a company that the owner basically threw away."

"Add Gil to the list," Finn instructed Siobhan. "I'll stop by to have a chat with him tomorrow. I understand his anger, but I also understand Tom's depression after his wife died. I would think Gil would understand as well."

"Maybe, but after a decade of working together, Tom ended up with a nice nest egg that he can live off while Gil ended up with nothing. I guess that his salary was adequate, but the real reason he devoted so much energy to the company was because Tom promised him a share of it when its assets reached a certain level. Before Tom's wife got sick, they were close. Now the retirement Gil counted on is nothing more than an unmet promise."

We continued to discuss potential suspects a while longer but didn't come up with any additional names to add, so Siobhan set the whiteboard aside, and the conversation segued to our plans for the upcoming holiday. Cody and I were in Florida last year at Christmas, as well as this year at Thanksgiving, so I was ready for a big family holiday. In addition to the huge Christmas Eve party we planned to throw at Mr. Parsons's house, I knew Siobhan planned to have the entire Hart family and an assortment of friends such as Tara and Sister Mary over for dinner on Christmas Day. Cody and I would have Sammy with us this year. As convinced as I was that motherhood was not for me—at least not yet—I was looking forward to having a baby to shop for this Christmas. Cody and I had discussed taking Sammy to see Santa and getting a photo to send to his parents, but that was before the explosion that seemed to have been the first in a series of events meant to ruin everyone's Christmas.

Chapter 5

Friday, December 13

I pulled on my running shoes, trying to be quiet so as not to wake Cody and Sammy. The baby had not slept through the night as we'd hoped, and Cody had been up walking him back and forth across the small living room for what seemed like hours. I'd offered to take over at one point, but Sammy really did prefer Cody, so we knew he had the best chance of getting him to nod off. Cody told me that he was grateful for the offer but suggested I go back to bed. I should feel a tad guiltier about the fact that going back to bed was exactly what I'd done, but it had been Cody who'd volunteered us for babysitting duty in the first place, so I supposed it was only right that he be the one to take on the majority of the sleepless nights.

Max and I exited the cabin through the kitchen door, and he ran down the beach while I settled into a relaxing jog. The sky was dark this morning, with angry-looking clouds. I'd love it if it snowed, but it wasn't all that cold, so it was likely if we got any precipitation it would be rain. Not that I minded rain. In fact, most of the time, I welcomed it. There was something about curling up in front of the fire in my little cabin while I watched the storm batter the dark sea.

As I passed Mr. Parsons's house, I found myself pausing. It was a pretty great house: three stories overlooking the sea. I was sure Cody and I would be very comfortable there, especially now that the remodel was done. The interior on the second and third floors where we'd be living had turned out amazing. Yet I still found myself resisting the move. Cody wanted us to be settled in prior to the Christmas Eve party we were throwing, and that made a lot of sense, but now that the time had come to actually make the move, I didn't know how I was going to say goodbye to my little cabin.

I glanced at the wall of windows on the top story. Mr. Parsons was quite happy living in just a few rooms on the first floor, and he fully supported us taking over both the second and third floors. Cody and I had decided on an open living space on the third floor, with the bedrooms and a small family room on the second. Right now, we didn't need a separate family room, but we realized that once we had children, we'd want a separate area for them to play when we had company.

Max looked impatient, so I continued on my way. I didn't need to look at the mansion to know that the top floor, with the huge open kitchen and dining area, large living room, and full bath, was spectacular. The area was about ten times as large as my cabin, so if we wanted to host the entire Hart family during some future Christmas, we had plenty of space in which to do it. There were five bedrooms on the second floor, including a master suite complete with a stone fireplace and a seating area, as well as the aforementioned family room and a home office for Cody.

But the house just didn't have the cozy feel of my little home. It wasn't right on the water the way my cabin was, nor did it contain the memories I'd been creating ever since Maggie had let me move into the cabin after I graduated high school.

By the time Max and I reached the end of the beach, where the sand turned into a rocky shore, it had started to sprinkle. I called Max and turned around, heading back in the direction from which we'd come. I tried to focus my attention on the beauty of the wintery day, but all I could think about was the impending end to a significant segment of my life. I got the fact that people moved every day, and I was moving into a really great house, but if I was honest with myself, I'd been dreading it ever since Cody had started talking about it.

"It's starting to rain," I said to Cody when Max and I returned to the cabin, entering the kitchen thought the side door.

"I heard we might get snow over the weekend. Not a lot, but enough to dust the ground."

I poured myself a cup of coffee "That would be nice. I love snow at Christmas." I glanced at Jingles, who was curled up in front of the fire. "Did he get his breakfast?"

"He did. Sammy has been fed as well, and I was just about to scramble myself a couple of eggs. Would you like some too?"

"I would. Thanks."

I'd left my sandy shoes outside the door, and now I padded across the floor in my stocking feet to give Max a scoop of dog food and refill his water dish before topping off my coffee. "So what are your plans for today?" I asked Cody.

"I'm going to take Sammy to the sitter's after we eat. I plan to spend the morning at the newspaper, and then I have a couple of guys coming by to help me start carrying the furniture we stored in the ballroom up to the second and third floors. I have a general idea of where you want things, but I figured you could move things around once we get the furniture in each room." Cody looked around the cabin. "Is there anything here you wanted to take with you?"

"I'm not sure. Cassie will need furniture, and you have plenty to get us started. I'm sure there are some personal things I'll want to bring with me. I'll give it some thought."

Cody poured the eggs into the skillet. "Just let me know what you want to take, and I'll move it over when you are ready." He popped bread in the toaster. "Did you want to do something this evening?"

I glanced at Sammy. "It's not like we can go out."

"Maybe we can pick up some Chinese food and watch a movie. We've been so busy that we've barely had time to enjoy the Christmas tree you took so much time with."

I glanced at the tree, as well as the lights along the mantel. "A cozy night in would be nice, and I did record a couple of Hallmark Channel Christmas movies we still need to watch. I should be home between five-thirty and six. I can pick up the food if you only plan to work half a day."

"How about I text you later, and we can work it out?" He set the food on the table.

As soon as Cody sat down, Sammy started to fuss. Cody started to get up.

"I'll get him," I offered.

"No, that's okay."

"You were up with him half the night. I guess it's my turn." I crossed the room and picked up the baby, and he stopped crying. Okay, that was a first. He normally would only stop crying if Cody picked him up.

"Your eggs will get cold," Cody warned.

"I can reheat them." I jiggled the baby a bit and then sat back down at the table with him in my arms. "He looks sort of flushed."

Cody frowned. He got up, walked around the table, and put a hand on his forehead. "He does feel warm. Maybe we should take him to the emergency room."

I brushed the baby's hair back from his face. "I'll call Siobhan. She's had a lot more baby experience than we have. She'll know if we should panic or wait it out."

Cody took the baby while I called Siobhan, who promised to come right over. Before she married Finn and they had Connor, I believed she'd be the Hart sibling never to marry or have children. She'd seemed so driven by her work, but then she reconnected with Finn, and everything changed.

"Just give him some of the infant Tylenol his mother sent with him, and keep an eye on his temperature," Siobhan suggested after she'd taken his temperature. "He only has a very mild fever. If it gets worse, then yeah, I'd take him to the ER."

"How much do I give him?" I asked, holding up the Tylenol box.

"The dosage is on the package. I'd keep him home, though. If he is coming down with something, it wouldn't be a good idea to take him to day care."

I glanced at Cody. "Fridays in December are really busy for us."

"I can work from home, and I'll reschedule the movers for next week. Sammy and I will be fine. You go ahead and go to work. Don't forget to get the Chinese food on the way home."

I thanked Siobhan and sent her on her way, and then went upstairs to shower and dress. I trusted Siobhan's advice. She was a great mother who took excellent care of Connor. But I couldn't help but worry about Sammy. He was so tiny. I hated to think that he wasn't feeling well.

When I came back down, Jingles was pacing and meowing. "What's with the cat?" I asked.

Cody shrugged. "I have no idea. He was sleeping, and then he jumped up and started pacing."

He had food and water and a clean litter box, so his basic needs had been met. "I'll take him with me. I have a feeling he is trying to tell me something."

"If he does lead you to a clue, don't go off sleuthing by yourself. Call Finn and let him follow up on it if that is even what the cat is after."

"I will." I leaned forward and kissed Cody on the lips. Sammy was in his arms, and he looked pretty happy and content now. "I'll call you later. If you need anything, call or text. If Sammy's fever goes up, and you decide to take him to the ER, I want to know right away."

"I will. Have a good day and remember, no sleuthing on your own."

"Yes, Dad," I teased. I knew Cody loved me and was only worried about my health and well-being, but sometimes he could be so overprotective. Of course, at times, I had ended up in some dicey situations, so maybe he was right to worry about me.

"Okay, what's the deal?" I asked the cat after we'd loaded into my car.

"Meow."

"It seems like you settled right down once you realized I was going to bring you with me. Did you just want to be sure I wouldn't leave you behind?"

"Meow."

"Yeah, I don't blame you. The kid has a set of lungs on him, that's for sure." I started the ignition. "My plan is to head to the bookstore, so if you want me to take a detour, you are going to need to let me know."

The cat curled up on the passenger seat. I pulled away from the estate and headed toward the peninsula road. It was possible the cat might still have something to show me, but maybe we were where we needed to be for him to point me in the right direction. When we arrived at the intersection where I would turn left to go into Pelican Bay, the seaside town where Coffee Cat Books was located, the cat jumped up and started howling.

"What is it?" I slowed and pulled over to the shoulder. "What do you want me to do?"

"Meow."

I looked toward my right. "Do you want me to turn right toward Sunset Beach?"

"Meow."

I hesitated and then did as the cat instructed. The road we'd turned onto led out to the beach and provided access to a housing area, but eventually, it came to a dead end. I wasn't sure why Jingles wanted me to go in that direction, but he seemed insistent, so I may as well see where he led me. When we got to the road that turned away from the beach toward the small housing development, he started yowling again, so I made the turn. The road eventually dead-ended at a yellow house with white shutters. Jingles got up and started clawing at the passenger side door. I stopped the vehicle.

"What now?" I asked.

He continued to claw at the door.

"What am I supposed to do? Go up to the house and tell whoever answers the door that my cat wants to check out their private, personal space?"

"Meow!"

I exhaled slowly. "Okay. Hang on." I took out my phone and called Finn.

"What's up?" he asked upon answering.

"Jingles brought me to a house out near Sunset Beach. I'm not sure what to do. He seems really insistent that we get out. I assume he wants us to check out the house."

Finn paused and then asked, "What street are you on?"

I looked around for a sign. "Sandy Way."

"Thirteen sixty-two?"

"Yup."

"That's Tom Miller's house. If the cat wants to go in, I think we should let him. Just wait in the car. I'll be there within fifteen minutes."

"Okay." I hung up and looked at the cat. "Finn is on his way. He said to wait."

The cat lay back down. I guess he was content with that answer. While we were waiting, I called Tara to let her know I'd be late getting into work. I hoped the ferry wasn't too full. If it was, she was going to have her hands full taking care of all those customers with only Cassie for help.

Thankfully, Finn arrived sooner than he'd estimated. He had a key to the house, which had been found along with other keys at the scene of the fire. I let the cat out of the car, and he ran up to the house. "Is it okay to go in?"

Finn nodded. "I have Tom's daughter's permission." Finn used the key to open the door, and we followed the cat inside.

The house was fairly messy, but I wouldn't say it was dirty. There were newspapers, discarded Christmas decorations, and a few items of clothing strewn around, but there weren't any dishes sitting around, and the trash cans had been recently emptied. We followed the cat into the kitchen, where we found a few dishes in the sink. The cat headed through the kitchen to the laundry room. He paused at a basket filled with dirty laundry.

I wrinkled my nose. "You want us to look through the man's laundry?"

"Meow."

Finn pulled on a pair of gloves. He took each item out of the basket, looking through the pockets if the garment had any, and then set it on the floor. About halfway down, he came to a pair of pants. Inside the pockets, he found four quarters, a small gold key, a piece of paper with a phone number written on it, and a bullet casing from a rifle.

"So, are we thinking the clue the cat wanted us to find is the key, the phone number, or the bullet casing?" I asked.

"I have no idea," Finn answered. "But I'd sure like to find out."

Chapter 6

When Jingles and I arrived at Coffee Cat Books, Tara and Cassie had their hands full. I dropped off Jingles in the cat lounge and then jumped in to help. While the bookstore portion of the enterprise did well, it was the coffee bar that kept us hopping. The fact that Coffee Cat Books was located on the wharf across from the ferry terminal had a lot to do with that. Folks would get off the ferry and walk across the wharf to grab a coffee and perhaps a muffin before heading into town to window-shop.

"Nonfat latte extra foam," the woman at the counter ordered.

I wrote down the instructions on the cup and then passed it on to Cassie, who was making the drinks. It appeared that Tara had been cornered in the bookstore by a customer who seemed to have a whole lot of questions about the new inventory.

"That'll be three seventy-five," I said.

The woman paid for her drink, and I looked toward the line to greet the next customer. "Alex," I greeted Alex Turner. "Are you going to work as our store Santa this year?"

I'd first met Alex five years ago when he'd applied for the job as our bookstore Santa. He'd not only become a close friend, but he was such a huge hit as Santa that we had him come back for a few days every year.

"I am." He smiled. "Tara wants me to be here afternoons from the eighteenth through the twenty-fourth."

"I'm looking forward to it. How is Willow feeling?" Willow was our part-time employee, who'd been out sick all week. She and Alex were raising her son together, and while they were about as close as any two people could be, the status of their relationship was somewhat undefined.

"She's feeling better. She hopes to be back to work next week. By the way, I heard about Chappy's boat. Is he okay?"

"He's fine," I assured Alex. "Both he and Cosmo were at O'Malley's when the fire started."

"That's good. After what happened to Tom, I was worried. I can't imagine who would have set fire to the Santa House. The whole thing is a tragedy."

"Finn, the gang, and I are working on a few theories. Did you know Tom well?"

"Not really. I ran into him from time to time, and we chatted. We both had roles as Santa, so we had that in common, but I can't say that we were close friends."

I glanced at the line behind Alex and realized we should wrap this up. "I'd love to chat with you about this further, but there is a line to deal with. Are you going to be in town for a while?"

"I have a couple of errands to take care of before I head back to the north shore. I could come back in about an hour."

"That would be perfect. And your coffee is on the house."

Alex left, and I greeted the next customer. It seemed that the line had only grown since I'd shown up. At least Tara was ringing up the customer she'd been helping with books, so maybe she could help Cassie and me, and between the three of us, we could get everyone taken care of.

"I just spoke to Carmen Simpson. She told me that it was Conway Granger who shot down the reindeer in town," Tara informed me as soon as she'd joined us at the coffee counter.

"Conway Granger burned down the Santa House too?"

"No. That's the surprising thing. We assumed all the vandalism that took place around town was connected to the fire at the Santa House, but it looks like the reindeer was an isolated incident."

"What happened?" I asked.

"According to Carmen, who works at Shots," Tara referred to a local bar, "Conway was in town on Wednesday singing the blues about this, that, and the other, and ended up having way too much to drink. When he left, he was driving that old truck of his, and one of his buddies decided to follow him home to make sure he'd make it safely. Apparently, the friend witnessed Conway pull over to the side of the road, grab his shotgun out of the truck, and shoot the reindeer overhead. Then he got back into his truck and drove home, where I guess he slept it off."

I handed the woman I'd been helping her change. "So why are we just finding this out now?"

"I guess the friend didn't want to cause any trouble for Conway, and Conway didn't even remember what he'd done, so no one said anything. But when word began to circulate that it was assumed the same person was responsible for the fire at the Santa House, the shooting of the reindeer, the vandalism to the nativity scene, the chopping down of the tree in the park, and the fire on Chappy's boat, the man figured he'd better speak up."

"Does Finn know about this?"

Tara nodded. "Carmen told me that Finn brought Conway in this morning. He has an alibi for the time of both the fire at the Santa House and the one on Chappy's boat. He admitted to being completely smashed on the night he shot the reindeer out of the sky and, as I said, he didn't even remember doing it. He didn't think he was responsible for the nativity scene or the Christmas tree in the park, but because he couldn't remember what he'd done that night, he couldn't be sure. However, the friend said that Conway went straight home after he shot Rudolph, so it looks like he is only on the hook for that."

I smiled at the last woman in line and took her order. Once Cassie had made the beverage and sent the woman on her way, I turned to Tara. "So it is possible that all the events happened independently?"

"I don't think so. Remember the mistletoe. It was found on Chappy's boat, at the nativity scene, and at the fallen tree in the park. I think we can assume that those three events are related. I have no idea if the person who did those things also burned the Santa House and killed Tom. I guess that will be up to Finn to unravel."

"I guess." I glanced at the clock. "Alex is coming back by. I wanted to speak to him about Tom and about the Christmas Eve party. He told me you'd already arranged for him to be Santa next week."

She nodded. "A lot of people have been asking about him. He sure is popular with the kids *and* their parents."

"He does have a way with people of all ages. I oftentimes wonder if he and Willow will settle down and build on the family they've started."

"Maybe someday."

The store was empty by the time Alex returned, so I suggested the two of us chat in the cat lounge. I started off by inviting him to the Christmas Eve party at Mr. Parsons's. He informed me that Mr. Parsons had already mentioned it, and both he and Willow planned to attend. I then asked him about Tom and whether he knew anything that might shed light on a motive for anyone to want him dead.

Alex paused, I assumed to consider my question. "So you think that the fire was directed at Tom specifically?"

"I'm not sure. It is possible that someone just wanted to burn down the Santa House and Tom was in the wrong place at the wrong time. But I think it would be a mistake not to at least consider that he was the target all along."

"I guess it makes sense that he could have been. Everyone knew Tom was the Santa on weekdays. I'm assuming the fire was set with some sort of a remote igniter?"

I nodded. "Someone planted a timer that set off a small explosion that started the fire which, according to Finn, was accelerated so that it would burn hot and fast."

"So the person who set the fire had experience in such things. It seems that to place a timer and to set up and control an explosion would take a certain amount of expertise. I certainly wouldn't know how to go about doing something like that. Would you?"

I frowned. "No. You make a good point. The majority of the population of Madrona Island probably couldn't have pulled it off."

"What about Gil Errington?" Alex suggested. "I know he was angry with Tom for closing down the business they built together the way he did, and he is ex-Army, so he probably could have pulled off the bomb."

"Gil's name has come up before, but why would he use the Santa House to kill Tom if he wanted him dead? If Tom was the target and didn't simply happen to be in the wrong place at the wrong time, why would the killer choose that particular method of eliminating him?"

Alex slowly shook his head. "No idea."

"Finn and I found some things in Tom's home. A key and a bullet casing from a rifle. Do either suggest anything to you?"

"No. Like I said, Tom and I chatted from time to time, but we weren't good friends or anything." He paused and drummed his fingers on the table. "I wonder if the bullet casing matches the rifle Conway just happened to have in his truck, which he used to shoot down the reindeer. Maybe the reindeer weren't the first casualty of his drunken hunting. Maybe he'd shot at other targets while on benders during the weeks before the reindeer were shot down. Maybe Tom happened to observe Conway during one of those drunken shooting sprees, and maybe Conway didn't want Tom telling anyone what he'd seen, so he killed him. At the very least, I'd match the bullet found in the reindeer with the casing found in Tom's house."

My eyes widened. "That's a good suggestion. I'll call Finn. The reindeer shooting occurred after Tom was dead, but you make a good point. Perhaps Conway was responsible for shooting something else before the fire at the Santa House."

Chapter 7

Jingles and I decided to check in with Finn before heading home for the evening. I'd called and spoken to Cody, who told me that Sammy was feeling much better and the slight fever he'd had that morning seemed to have broken. He was looking forward to eating Chinese takeout and watching a movie by the fire this evening, and I promised to be home as soon as I was able. I knew Finn liked to get home to Siobhan and Connor by dinnertime as well, so I would make our conversation a quick one.

"So, did the bullet found inside the reindeer match the casing found in Tom's pocket?" I asked the minute I entered Finn's office.

"It did not, but the bullet inside the reindeer and the casing in Tom's pocket were from a similar rifle, just not the same one. I'm not sure the casing is important, but it might be, so I'm going to keep my eye out for other incidents involving hunting rifles."

I sat down across from Finn while Jingles chose to jump up on his desk and settle down on top of a stack of file folders. "And the phone number?"

"Unfortunately, that didn't match any number that would be used with our local area code, and there was no area code on the piece of paper, so at this point, the number is fairly useless. I'm still working on it, but figuring out whose number Tom wrote down won't be as easy as just dialing it. I still have no idea what the key goes to, and the quarters, while old, don't seem to be anything special."

"Old? How old?"

"All four quarters were minted between 1932 and 1935. The first year was the first one in which the Washington quarter was minted. They all look to be uncirculated, so I have to assume Tom got them from a collector. While it is sort of interesting that he had coins dating back more than eighty years that had never been used, they aren't hugely valuable, so I doubt they could provide a motive for murder."

"So, are we looking at things any differently now that we know Conway was responsible for Rudolph's fall from the sky?"

Finn slowly shook his head. "Not really. We never were certain that all the events were related. I do think the tree in the park, the nativity scene, and Chappy's boat are connected because of the mistletoe. And I suspect we'll find that the person responsible for these deeds is also responsible for the burning of the Santa House, but I won't go so far as to say that is a given. If you stop to think about it, the crimes are all different. Even if Tom hadn't been at the Santa House and hadn't died in the fire, the fire there seems a lot more violent to me than cutting down a tree in the park."

"Even if the tree that was cut down is the same one the community has used as its Christmas tree since before I was born?"

"Even then."

"I do see what you're saying, although the fire on Chappy's boat and the fire at the Santa House were both fires."

"True," Finn agreed. "But the one at the Santa House was designed to destroy the entire structure quickly and completely. The one on Chappy's boat seemed designed to be seen and dealt with before total destruction would occur. Think about it: an accelerant was used at the Santa House to make sure it burned hot and fast, but the fire on Chappy's boat, while cruel, was actually very small, and it was set during a time of day when it would be noticed and dealt with before any major damage occurred. It was also set when it was known that Chappy would be out. I almost wonder if that second fire wasn't simply a diversion from the true intention behind the first one."

"Okay, say that's true. Why Chappy's boat? I understand that the second fire resulted in the loss of Christmas decorations, which sent us down the path of looking for a Grinch who was trying to destroy the popular holiday, but why Chappy's boat? Why not set fire to the decorations at the community center or the gazebo in the park with its North Pole display?"

Finn exhaled. "I don't know. Maybe the fire at Chappy's boat was personal."

"Which would mean whoever did this was known to Chappy."

"Perhaps."

"This whole thing is making me nervous. When I spoke to Tansy, she made it sound like there might be more than one thing going on. She warned me not to be diverted."

"I guess she was right. There is more than one thing happening. We already know that the reindeer incident isn't related to anything else. Maybe there are just a bunch of random acts of vandalism going on, and maybe none of them are connected. I imagine time will tell."

I stood up. "I need to get home. It's takeout-and-movie night."

"Siobhan told me Sammy had a fever. How is the little guy doing?"

"Cody said he's better," I answered. "Taking care of a baby is hard. I don't know how people do it."

"When it is your own baby, you develop a routine. I was scared to death when I first found out I was going to be a father. Happy, but scared. What if I was terrible at it? What if the fact that Siobhan and I both had demanding jobs created an adverse environment for the child? But I think things are working out just fine. When you and Cody are ready to start your own family, you'll figure it out as well. In the meantime, enjoy Sammy. What you are doing for him is really important. Babies need to feel loved and secure, and I know you and Cody are the best temporary parents the little guy could ever ask for."

Finn was right about Cody being an awesome temporary father, but I wasn't so sure that I was equally awesome as a temporary mother.

The Chinese restaurant Cody and I favored was in Harthaven, so after I left Finn's office, Jingles and I went in that direction. The sun set early at this time of the year, so it was already dark. I was hoping the snow everyone kept talking about would arrive, but so far, all we've had to show for the heavy, dark clouds were a few sprinkles of rain throughout the day.

I slowed as I entered the main downtown section of town. The merchants had done a wonderful job with the decorations this year. Every lamppost had a wreath, every window a seasonal display, and every building and patio tree a string or two of white lights.

The restaurant didn't have its own parking area, but there was a spot on the street not far from it, so I pulled into it before anyone else could grab it out from under me. Normally, the little town wasn't all that busy after dark during the off-season, but with Christmas just around the corner, a lot of folks were out shopping and running errands.

"Okay, you'll need to wait here," I said to Jingles. "I'll just be a few minutes."

"Meow."

"I'll see if I can order a plain chicken breast for you and Max to share. Now be good, and don't claw the upholstery."

Jingles lay down, seemingly content to wait, so I exited the car, locked it, and walked quickly down the half of block separating me from my destination. I placed the order, texted Cody to give him an update on my ETA, and waited. As I did, three other customers came in, one of them was Tara's ex-boyfriend, Dr. Parker Hamden, apparently with a date.

"Parker. How are you?" I gave the man, who at one point I thought Tara might end up married to, a hug.

"I'm good. How are you?"

"Good. Cody and I are having takeout."

Parker turned to the woman on his arm. "This is Lorana Fowler. Lorana, this is Cait Hart."

"I'm happy to meet you," I said to the other woman.

"You own the bookstore," Lorana said.

"I do. Along with my friend, Tara. Have you been in?"

"I have, and it's wonderful. I especially love the little village. There has been so much attention given to detail that it feels like a real place."

"That's all Tara. She has added to the village every year. Our customers really seem to enjoy coming in to see what's new." I glanced at Parker. He had a scowl on his face. I guess I didn't blame him. Tara had broken up with him despite the fact that things between them had seemed to be going well. I guess I could see why he wasn't thrilled that I was jabbering on about her and her magical Christmas Village. "How's Amy?" I asked Parker, referring to his niece.

"She's good. Excited for the upcoming holiday." He looked toward the restaurant. "It was nice seeing you, but we're meeting some friends. We should find them."

"It was good seeing you as well. And Lorana, it was good meeting you."

I smiled as the couple walked away, but deep down, I had to acknowledge that had been awkward. I still wasn't entirely sure why Tara had broken up with

Parker. She'd said that they just hadn't shared that special spark, and maybe that was true, but they'd gotten along well and he seemed to treat her right. Tara hadn't gone into any detail when I asked about her decision to end the relationship, but I suspected the real reason was that, despite all the starts and stop and ups and downs, the spark she referred to was something she had only ever shared with Danny.

"Your order is up," the cashier announced.

I thanked him, slipped him a tip, and headed back to my car. When I arrived, I found Jingles outside sitting on a bench with a young mother and her son. How on earth had the cat gotten out of the car? I was sure I'd locked it.

"How did you get out of the car?" I asked Jingles.

"Meow."

"Is this your cat?" the woman asked.

"Sort of. I left him in the car while I went in to pick up takeout. I don't know how he got out. Is he bothering you?"

"Just the opposite." The woman smiled. "This is my son, Wiley. He's autistic and doesn't usually like animals, but this cat walked right up to him, and he bent down to greet him like a long-lost friend. I was sort of hoping he was a stray who needed a home. Wiley could use a friend to bond with."

I glanced at the boy, who was staring into the eyes of the cat. Jingles was purring and staring back. It almost looked as if they were communicating telepathically.

"Jingles is staying with me for the time being. We are working on a project together, but there is a good chance he will be eligible for adoption when the project is over. If you want to give me your number, I can call you when he becomes eligible, and we can discuss the situation further."

"I'd like that very much." The woman pulled a piece of paper from her purse. She jotted down a number. "I know it looks like a long-distance number, but it is a cell. I got the phone when I lived on the East Coast and never changed the number."

I glanced at it. "Okay, great. Just so you know, I own Coffee Cat Books along with my business partner, Tara. I'm there most of the time when the store is open if you need to reach me."

"Okay. Perfect." She bent down and scratched Jingles under the chin. "I'm so happy you found us, and I can't wait to welcome you into the family."

"Meow."

From the loud purr accompanying the exchange, I was willing to bet that Jingles was excited about becoming a member of the family too.

Chapter 8

Monday, December 16

It had been a long weekend. I'd left on the first ferry of the morning the day before and had driven into Seattle to pick up the cats I planned to rescue from the high kill shelter. Once I returned to the island, I spent a couple of hours getting them settled into the cat sanctuary. Two of them were pregnant moms, so I had to make sure they had a safe and nurturing place to deliver their babies.

By the time that was done, it was late afternoon, but I still pitched in to help Cody begin moving our stuff into Mr. Parsons's place. I had to admit that when Monday morning rolled around, I was actually happy to have something else to focus my attention on. Coffee Cat Books was closed on Mondays, but with the rush of holiday shoppers, Tara and I had decided to come in to restock the shelves and do the cleaning that had been neglected during the previous week when the store had been bursting at the seams with customers.

"I ran into Parker on Friday night when I stopped off to pick up Chinese food," I said as casually as I could manage.

"Oh? How is he?"

"He seemed fine. He was out for dinner with a woman named Lorana."

Tara used the box cutter to slit the top of the next box. "That's nice. I've met her a time or two. She seems like a nice woman." She looked into the box and began sifting the objects inside around. "Have you seen the ski lift I ordered for the Christmas Village? It should be here by now."

"I saw a box with an ice-skating rink, but no ski lift. I'll let you know if I find it." I set the box I'd been unpacking aside and opened the next one. "Seeing Parker made me wonder why it didn't work out between the two of you. It seemed like you got along okay."

"We got along wonderfully. I told you that before. There just wasn't any spark. I knew Parker was looking to find a woman to settle down with, and I was never going to be that woman, so despite the fact that I enjoyed spending time with him, I decided to let him go." Tara reached into a box and pulled out a tall mechanical ski lift. "I found it. Now keep an eye out for the skiers I ordered to accent the lift."

"So, by spark you mean chemistry?" I wasn't sure why I wasn't just letting this go.

Tara shrugged. "I guess. Sort of. What it came down to was that while I liked Parker and had a lot of fun with him, and I enjoyed spending time with Amy, I wasn't in love with him. At first, I kept thinking the love would come once the friendship deepened, but it never happened." She glanced at the box I'd pulled off the pile. "I think those are the new mugs. You can put as many as will fit on the shelf and then leave the box behind the counter. I think we'll need to restock often as soon as our customers see how cute they are."

I opened the box and pulled one out. "They are cute. I may have to take one home, wherever home might be at this moment in time."

"Are you still in transition?"

I nodded. "Cody made a lot of progress over the weekend. We could begin staying over at Mr. Parsons's now if we wanted to. In fact, most of my stuff is already over there. I'm just not sure I'm ready to cut the strings completely. In fact, when I think of officially turning my little cabin over to Cassie, all I want to do is to lock myself inside and tell everyone to go away."

"It is a pretty great cabin. But the new place is pretty great as well."

"It is an awesome place, and there is plenty of room to grow, but it doesn't feel like home. When I'm over there, I appreciate the awesome view and the upgraded interior, but I feel like a visitor in someone else's home. I know this move makes sense for a lot of reasons. Mentally, I've made the decision to go, but I'm having a hard time letting go emotionally."

Tara paused what she was doing. "I think that is understandable. I'd say keep the cabin for a while even after you make the move next door, but I know Cassie is waiting to move in. I guess the only advice I have is for you to bite the bullet, make the move, and then work on making the place feel like home."

I picked up the half-empty box of mugs and carried it behind the counter. "I know you're right. And I will do what I've already promised Cody and Cassie I would do. It's just turned out to be harder than I thought it would."

"Can you look in that box over by the door to see if the bookmarks we ordered are inside it?"

I did as Tara asked. "This box has both bookmarks and postcards," I informed her.

"Okay, great. I think the box with the cute little Christmas stockings is still in the back. I want to hang a few from the shelves, and then I thought we'd put the rest in a basket near the cash register. I'm hoping our customers will want to add one to their order when they check out."

"I'll get the box," I offered.

I headed toward the storage room at the back of the shop. Tara usually kept it perfectly organized, but it had been busy, and boxes had been left in the middle of the room waiting to be unpacked. It took me a few minutes to find the stockings Tara was looking for, but eventually, I did and carried it to the front.

"Cassie," I greeted my younger sister when I got there. "What are you doing here on your day off?"

Cassie plucked a piece of candy from the jar on the counter and popped it into her mouth. "I was in town having breakfast with some friends, and someone came in and told everyone about the toy store. I wondered if you'd heard."

"Toy store?" I asked. "What about the toy store?"

"The toy store in Harthaven was vandalized last night," Cassie informed me. "It seems someone pulled everything off the shelves, damaging some things in the process."

"The Grinch strikes again," Tara said.

"I think so," Cassie agreed. "I heard that the cash register was stuffed full of mistletoe."

"So, that makes the nativity scene, the Christmas tree in the park, the fire on Chappy's boat, and the toy store that have been vandalized by the person I'm beginning to think of as the mistletoe vandal," I said.

"What about the reindeer over Main Street?" Tara asked.

"I found out that the reindeer were shot down by Conway Granger on a bender," I informed the others. "From what I've heard, he actually thought they were real reindeer flying overhead when he saw them, so he pulled out his rifle and shot them."

"That's crazy," Cassie said. "What if he'd shot a real animal or a person?"

"Yeah, he must have been hammered. I'm not sure what Finn did with him, but I'm sure there will be consequences, not only for inflicting damage on town property but for discharging a firearm within the town limits and for driving drunk, which he had been."

"So, did Finn ever figure out if this mistletoe vandal is also responsible for burning down the Santa House?" Cassie asked.

"He wasn't sure the last time I spoke to him," I answered. "There wasn't any mistletoe to be found at the scene of the Santa House, but of course, the building was a total loss, so even if there had been some left, it would have been burned to a crisp in the fire."

"I just don't understand why the mistletoe vandal wants to ruin everyone's Christmas," Cassie said. "Even if the poor guy at the toy store has insurance to cover the damage, he is going to lose the revenue normally generated during the busiest couple of weeks of the year."

"Tansy mentioned that she was able to connect with someone in great pain. I'm not sure if she was channeling the person who burned down the Santa House or the mistletoe vandal if they aren't the same person," I said.

"Or maybe she was connecting with someone else altogether," Tara said. She stood up from where she was kneeling on the floor looking through a box. She glanced around the room. "Did you find the new paperbacks we ordered?"

"They are over by the coffee bar," Cassie said. "I'll put them on the new-arrivals rack."

"You really don't have to. This is your day off," Tara reminded her.

She shrugged. "I know. And I'm not going to stay long. I'm just hanging out while my friend, Rosalie, drops off her sister at the day care center." She picked up a book on grief. "Does anyone know if Finn ever talked to Clifford Little? It seems like Cliff is as good a candidate to be the mistletoe vandal as any after losing his wife and son at Christmas."

"I spoke to Finn about Cliff," I answered. "He was off the island on the day the Santa House burned up. Of course, that doesn't totally let him off the hook because a timer set off the explosion that ignited the fire. Yet, while it is possible that Cliff set up the bomb before leaving the island, Finn also said that generally speaking, arsonists like to watch the destruction they cause."

"I saw something about that on TV," Tara shared.

"And the brother-in-law?" Cassie asked.

"I'm not sure," I answered. "I guess I should check in with Finn today. Cody and I were so busy moving this weekend that I never had a chance to see how his investigation was going."

Cassie's face lit up. "Moving? Does that mean I will be able to move into the cabin soon?"

I wanted to say no. "Just give me a couple of days, and the place will be all yours."

Cassie clapped her hands together and then jumped into the air, letting out a small screech of joy. I supposed knowing that I was making my baby sister that happy softened the blow of saying goodbye to the home I loved just a bit.

Chapter 9

"I think we've done what we needed to today." Tara pushed her hands into her lower back to relive an ache there. "I'm going to head over to O'Malley's for a glass of wine. Want to come?"

I lifted a shoulder. "Yeah. I could use some wine. I should probably go home to finish packing my personal possessions, as I promised Cassie I would, but a glass of wine with my best friend seems like the less emotionally charged choice."

"Maybe the wine will help you relax so when you get home you can tackle the packing."

"I'll probably need more than one glass to accomplish that, but I do get what you are saying. I'm just going to text Cody to let him know where I'll be."

As most of the other businesses on the island had done, O'Malley's went all out with their holiday décor. I suspected Tara might have helped; while I could see my brothers decorating the tree in the corner, I couldn't picture them draping real pine garlands from the bar or hanging hundreds of white twinkle lights overhead.

When we walked in, Danny smiled, although it seemed to be directed at Tara, not both of us, and she smiled back. While they had dated and even entered into moderately serious relationships with other people since they'd last been a couple, there was no use denying they had spark.

"The place looks great," I said to Danny, who stood behind the bar. "I especially love the beer-drinking Santa by the front door."

"The Santa was Tara's idea, but the beer was mine. You want a glass of wine?"

"Please. White."

"Tara?" Danny asked.

"I'll have some of the Syrah you gave me last night. It was really good."

So, the two of them had been together last night? Interesting. The bar was closed on Sundays, so I didn't think they were here. Not that it was any of my business. Exactly. Although we were talking about a coupling between my best friend and my brother. A coupling, I reminded myself, that seemed like a very bad idea to me.

"Where's Aiden?" I asked.

"He's off today. I think he said something about heading to Seattle for Christmas shopping."

I groaned. "I haven't even started mine. I really should get on that with Christmas practically around the corner. It's just with Sammy and the move and all, it really has been hectic."

"Mom wants a new computer," Danny said. "The one she has keeps freezing. Aiden and I were going to go in on one together. Do you want in on the action?"

"I do," I answered. One gift down, a bunch more to go.

"Aiden was going to pick it up. He knows more about them than I do. Once he gets it and I know how much it cost, I'll let you know what your share comes out to."

"Did you remember to order the wine we talked about for the Christmas Eve party?" I asked.

"I did. It should be here by the end of the week. I'm going to take it over to Mr. Parsons's place, so it doesn't get mixed up with the bar's inventory. By the way, I took a tour of the remodel when I stopped by to chat with Cody this weekend. It's really nice. I bet you are excited to get moved in."

"Yeah. Real excited."

"Did you hear about the vandalism at the toy store?" Tara asked Danny, changing the subject. If I had to guess, she'd done that intentionally to forestall the whole moving conversation.

"I did," Danny answered. "Finn stopped by for lunch. He says the place was a real mess."

I nodded. "It does sound like the mistletoe vandal was busy last night."

Danny took out a bottle of whiskey and poured himself a shot. "Finn shared with me that he is confused by the whole thing. Normally, if a single person carries out a series of crimes, whether it be murder, vandalism, theft, or whatever, the severity can escalate over time. But with the ones we've been witnessing on the island, the burning of the Santa House was the most severe of all, and it came first.

The pattern feels off to him. Someone destroys an entire building, killing someone in the process, then goes out and cuts down a tree, steals baby Jesus from a nativity scene, and then starts a very small fire on Chappy's boat. Why? Even more curious is the fact that whoever it is seems to go goes dormant for a few days, and then jumps back in with a big mess at the toy store. Finn felt the sequence was off, and I agreed it made very little sense."

"What about the theory we discussed at the Scooby meeting in which the guy who burned down the Santa House did the other stuff to divert attention from his real activity?" Tara said.

"Yeah, it could be that way," Danny said. "If Tom was the target all along. But why trash the toy store after being quiet for a few days?"

"Did Finn say whether he was getting anywhere with the case?" I asked.

"Not really. He's talked to a lot of people. Some he's cleared after obtaining their alibi, others he's left on his suspect list pending further investigation. He is trying to track down the source of the mistletoe. There are several places selling it on the island. So far, none of the vendors he's spoken to remembers selling it to anyone who asked for a large quantity. Most customers buy one or two pieces, so anyone buying four or more would stand out."

"I suppose the mistletoe vandal might have purchased it off the island," I said.

"I think that is the conclusion Finn has come to."

Tara took a sip of her wine. She set down the glass and ran a finger along the rim. "If we take the fire at the Santa House out of the picture, the fire on Chappy's boat stands out to me as being the odd man out. The vandalism of the nativity scene took place at Saint Patrick's, which is in Harthaven. The tree that was cut down was in the park, which is in Harthaven. The trashing of the toy store also took place in Harthaven. All three happened at night when no one was around, but the fire on Chappy's boat took place at the marina in Pelican Bay, and in the middle of the day. It doesn't fit the pattern."

I frowned. "You do have a good point." I looked at Danny. "Is Chappy back living on his boat?"

"He is," Danny confirmed. "The boat itself suffered very little damage. Only his decorations were the worse for wear. Though if you hadn't seen the smoke when you did, the boat could have been a total loss. Chappy was lucky."

Yes, he was lucky, but I still had to agree with Tara that the fire on the boat didn't fit with the other acts of vandalism. Even the fire at the Santa House took place in Harthaven, although it did happen in the middle of the day.

"I guess Finn must not have recovered any physical evidence at any of the scenes," Tara said.

Danny shook his head. "He dusted for prints, but all the targets were public locations with lots of traffic, so there were a lot of prints. He didn't find anything that stood out as being significant. Other than the mistletoe, he didn't find any sort of physical evidence that seemed to be evident at all the locations."

"It seems to me that someone must have seen something at some point," Tara said. "Especially Chappy's boat. Based on the small amount of damage, the fire must have been set within minutes of Cait spotting the smoke. It almost seems as if the person who set the fire should have still been hanging around."

"I don't remember seeing anyone," I said. "But I do agree with what you just said. It seems as if at the very least I would have passed the arsonist leaving as I approached along the wharf."

"Unless the guy didn't leave," Danny said.

I raised a brow. "Didn't leave? If he didn't leave, I would have seen him."

"Not if he set the fire and then hopped onto one of the other boats in the marina. There are still a handful of houseboats left."

Danny made another good point. It did seem likely that whoever set the fire on Chappy's boat had been close by to see how it all turned out. If he set the fire and then disappeared below the deck of a nearby boat, he could keep an eye on things without being seen.

"Who owns the boat two slips over from Chappy's?" I asked, knowing that the slip right next to Chappy's was vacant.

"I'm not sure offhand, but I can make a call and find out."

As it turned out, a businessman who lived in Seattle but had a weekend home on the island to Chappy's owned the boat closest to Chappy's. He was not on the island when the fire was set, but that didn't mean that whoever started the fire hadn't hopped on board to hide out on it. The vessel had a large living area below deck, which would have provided the perfect place to keep an eye on the fire he'd set on Chappy's boat and avoid being seen.

Danny had to stay at the bar because Aiden wasn't there to cover, and Tara indicated that she planned to stay and have dinner there, but I decided to stop by the marina on my way home. The boat docked closest to Chappy's was a large vessel. Older, but it appeared to be serviceable. I stood on the dock looking between the two boats. I didn't necessarily expect to find anything, but I felt compelled to look.

"You lookin' for me?" Chappy asked from his own deck.

I smiled at the old sea captain. "Not really. I was chatting with Danny and Tara at the bar, and it occurred to us that whoever set the fire on your boat must still have been at the marina when I showed up. We figured that he must have hidden on a nearby boat to watch what happened. I hoped to notice something that would prove that theory."

"No need to look any further. I figured out who set the fire on my boat. I confronted them, and we worked things out."

"Who was it?" I asked.

"I'd rather not say."

"But the same person who set fire to your boat is most likely the one who vandalized the nativity scene at the church and cut down the tree in the park and trashed the toy store and possibly burned down the Santa House."

"Weren't the same person."

I narrowed my gaze. "How can you be sure?"

"The person who started the fire on my boat had a grudge against me. She got the idea for the fire from the Santa House, but I can assure you, she didn't burn that down."

"She?"

His eyes widened. "Or he. Either way. The individual who set fire to my boat wasn't involved in any of the other things that happened on the island. I can promise you as much."

"What about the mistletoe? There was mistletoe on your boat, and there was mistletoe left at the nativity scene at the church, the park, and the toy store."

"I asked about that, and she—or he," he qualified, "told me that a friend had told her about the mistletoe, so she decided to buy some and leave it as a false clue."

Okay, from all Chappy's stumbles, I knew the person who'd set the fire on his boat was a female. I would say she was a scorned lover, but Chappy was too old to be anyone's lover. Wasn't he? "Are you absolutely sure that the person who set fire to your boat didn't set fire to the Santa House, or chop down the tree in the park, or vandalize the nativity scene at the church, or trash the toy store?"

He nodded. "Yes. I am absolutely certain the fire on my boat is not connected to any of the other things that happened on the island."

I could see that Chappy wasn't going to tell me the name of the woman who'd gotten so angry with him that she'd burned up all his Christmas decorations, so I nodded and then turned to leave. I figured I could mention this to Finn and let him play the bad guy and interrogate Chappy. I took a step toward the wharf and then looked back. "You said the person who started a fire on your boat heard about the mistletoe from someone else. But the fire on your boat was set only four of five hours after Finn discovered the mistletoe, so it wasn't widely known. How did your friend know about it?"

"She, or he," he said in a lame attempt to keep up the pretense, "as the case may be, told me that she, or he, had heard about the mistletoe found at the site where the tree was chopped down from the guy who sells mistletoe from that little stand by the park. In fact, she told me that it was from this man that she bought the mistletoe she left on my boat."

I tilted my head just a bit. "What did you do to make this woman so angry that she would go to all the trouble of burning up your decorations?"

Chappy smiled a crooked grin. "A man's love life is not the sort of thing that should be discussed with a youngin like yourself."

Chapter 10

Tuesday, December 17

Siobhan had decided to work from home today, so she offered to watch Sammy so I wouldn't have to take him to the sitters. Maggie and Michael had returned home, although they planned to be back for a week at Christmas, and Cassie was working at the bookstore, so Siobhan would be alone with both Connor and Sammy. I asked her if she felt she could handle two babies, to which she laughed and said, of course, she could. My big sister really was amazing.

"Did Finn already leave for work?" I asked her after entering the main house through the kitchen.

"He left hours ago."

"Did he have a chance to speak to the mistletoe vendor in the park?" I had to admit I was still curious as to the identity of Chappy's lady friend.

"He did. According to him, only one woman bought a sprig of mistletoe from him the morning after the tree in the park was cut down and that was Valda Cameron."

My eyes widened. "Valda Cameron? Are you sure?"

Siobhan nodded.

While Chappy was a weathered fisherman whose rough lifestyle had left him physically worse for wear, Valda was a classy and sophisticated woman in her early fifties who earned a good income from the boutique she owned.

"No matter how hard I try, I can't imagine the two of them together."

Siobhan picked Connor up and set him in his playpen. "Finn spoke to Valda, who told him that she'd heard a rumor that Chappy had been making eyes at a couple of the women from the senior quilting circle when they came into the bar for lunch on Thursdays. She confronted him about it, expecting that he'd tell her he only had eyes for her, but instead, he mentioned one of the women specifically, who'd worn a red sweater and jingle bell earrings to lunch that day. He admitted to being drawn to her, but he told Valda not to worry because it was only the fact that she looked like a Christmas decoration that had gotten his attention. Valda admitted to being so angry she couldn't see straight. After stewing on things for a few days, she found herself so enraged that she went to Chappy's boat to break up with him, but when she got there, he was gone. She realized that not only had he gone to the bar for lunch early that day, but that it was Thursday, and the 'Christmas floozy,' as she referred to Chappy's crush, would be there. That only made her madder."

"Valda used the term 'Christmas floozy'?" I grinned.

"According to Finn. Anyway, she noticed the pile of Christmas decorations Chappy had left on the table and in a fit of rage, she set them on fire."

I laughed out loud at this point. "This whole thing is just so bizarre. I understand the woman's anger, but what if I hadn't seen the smoke? What if Chappy's boat had burned up?"

Siobhan shrugged. "Valda said she was keeping an eye on the fire. It would most likely have just burned itself out even if you hadn't come along."

"So how does the mistletoe fit into this?"

"Before coming to visit Chappy, Valda stopped at the mistletoe vendor in the park to buy some for the entry of her home. While she was there, he mentioned that mistletoe was left at the scene of the tree vandalism. After she started the fire on the boat, she realized she had the mistletoe she'd purchased in her purse, so, on impulse, she decided to leave it there. She realized later that was probably a mistake, but she admitted that at the time she set the fire she was just so dang mad she wasn't thinking straight."

I picked up a piece of apple from the tray of fruit Siobhan was slicing. "Did Finn arrest Valda?"

"No. They talked it out, and she understands that what she did was wrong. Chappy didn't want to press charges, and Finn didn't want to get into the middle of a lovers' spat, so he's going to leave things alone."

"Is he sure that the fire on Chappy's boat was the only incident Valda was responsible for?"

Siobhan transferred the apple slices into a bowl. "He seemed fairly sure. The guy who sold Valda the mistletoe pointed out that he secures his sprigs with red ribbon. The mistletoe found at the toy store, the nativity scene, and the Christmas tree had been tied with dark green ribbon. Apparently, most vendors use slightly different ribbon. The dark green looks to have come from one on San Juan Island. Finn headed over there on the first ferry so he could chat with him and still get back here in time to follow up on any information that might be provided to him."

"It'd be crazy if Finn was able to solve these acts of vandalism based on ribbon color."

"More often than not, it really is some seemingly minor detail that blows cases wide open," Siobhan pointed out.

"Is he still thinking the fire in the Santa House is unrelated to the other incidents?" I asked.

"So far that is his theory, although the fact that two of the acts of vandalism have turned out to be unrelated to the others does seem to put a twist in the idea that the other, lesser ones are all related. I guess he'll just need to continue to approach each crime in isolation and then see where he ends up. If all goes well and one of the mistletoe vendors can identify the person who purchased the mistletoe with the green ribbon, he might at least get part of these incidents wrapped up."

I picked up a piece of pear as Siobhan turned her attention to the next fruit she'd lined up on the counter for slicing. "I wish I could stay to see how it all works out, but I need to get to work. Call me if Finn is able to ID the mistletoe vandal."

"I will."

"And thanks for watching Sammy. Two seems like a lot to take on at once, but I suppose this will be good practice for when you decide to give Connor a little brother or sister."

"Exactly. Finn and I have started talking about another baby. I'm not sure we're ready quite yet, but time goes by so fast. You need to stay on top of those things."

I thought about what Siobhan had said as I walked back to my cabin to grab my purse. I supposed she had a point about staying on top of things, but how did one know if or when they were ready to be a parent? The whole idea seemed to me to be completely overwhelming.

I opened the door to my cabin and was greeted by Jingles. Cody had taken Max to work with him, as he often did, so the cat would be alone unless I brought him with me. "Do you want to come to the bookstore with me?"

"Meow." He ran across the room, jumped up onto the kitchen counter, grabbed something in his mouth, then jumped down, ran back to me, and set a piece of paper at my feet. I looked down to see what he'd brought me. "It's the phone number for the woman who wants to adopt you. I know you really hit it off with her son and are anxious to get settled into your forever home, but I can't let you go until we solve Tom's murder. I assume you are here to solve Tom's murder and not to find the mistletoe vandal because I'm pretty much convinced we are looking for two different people at this point."

"Meow." He trotted over to the door and began to scratch at it.

"Were you even listening to me?"

The cat trotted back over, took a paw, and shoved the piece of paper closer to me.

I bent over and picked it up. I supposed the cat might have a different reason for wanting me to call the woman, but I had no idea what it might be. Still, the worst thing that could happen if I called her and explained that Jingles had insisted I do it would be that she'd think I was a total loon.

"Okay. I'll call her. But if she decides she doesn't want to adopt you after this, it won't be my fault."

"Meow."

I dialed the number. "Hi. This is Cait Hart. With the cat."

"Is he eligible for adoption?"

"No," I answered. "Not quite yet. But he did seem insistent that I call you. I'm not sure why."

"He must somehow know that Wiley has been upset all morning. I've tried everything to calm him down, but he is more agitated than I've seen him in a long time. Maybe you could bring the cat over? If not to leave him for good, at least for a visit."

I looked at the cat, who was sitting by the door. "Okay. Yeah, I could do that. Just give me your address."

I called Tara to let her know I'd be late yet again, put the cat in a carrier, and headed toward Harthaven. I was aware the cat and the child had connected somehow the minute they met. Maybe Jingles really had sensed that the boy needed him.

When I arrived at the address the woman had given me, I took the cat out of the carrier and headed toward the front door. I noticed immediately that the house backed on the park. The same park where the Santa House had been before it burned to the ground.

"Thank you so much," the woman said as soon as she opened the door. "My name is Jane, by the way. I'm not sure I introduced myself when we met. Wiley has been beside himself ever since we took a walk this morning and I'm not sure what I can do to calm him down."

The boy came down the stairs, and the cat wiggled out of my arms. He ran straight over to the boy, who fell to his knees. The cat and Wiley stared into each other's eyes for a moment, and then the boy ran upstairs. Jingles followed.

"Come on in," Jane said. "Let me get you some coffee, and then I'll go check on them."

"Thanks. I'd appreciate that. I see noticed your property backs on the park."

"Yes. It works out well because I can take Wiley out walks before it gets crowded. He doesn't always do well with crowds. I took him out this morning, and he seemed to have extra energy to burn, so I looped around and brought him back home past where the Santa House burned. It was a mistake. When we arrived there, he went a little crazy. And now he's been a little crazy all morning."

I glanced up as I heard footprints on the stairs. Wiley came into the room with Jingles on his heels. He handed his mother a piece of paper that looked as if it was torn from a sketchbook. His mother took it from him.

"Wiley likes to draw. It is one of the ways he can communicate with me because he doesn't speak."

"What did he draw?"

She turned the paper around. The drawing was of Santa Claus standing in the doorway of a burning building.

"Do you think he saw what happened?" I asked.

"No. We were at home the day of the fire, not in the park."

"Is this the Santa House?" I asked him.

The boy's eyes never met mine, but he sat down on the floor and quickly began drawing with a pencil. After a moment, he held up the paper. This time he'd drawn the inside of the Santa House. Santa was sitting in his chair and next to him was a package all wrapped up like a Christmas present.

"Santa on his throne," I said.

The boy still hadn't looked directly at me, but he took his pencil and scribbled out the present. Then he drew flames coming from it.

"Are you saying a present caused the fire?" I asked.

Again, he didn't look at me, but the cat let out a long meow.

I turned to Jane. "It has been determined that the fire was caused by a small explosion that set off a spark that ignited an accelerant. The house went up quickly, with Santa inside. Are you sure he couldn't have somehow been a witness to what happened?"

"Trust me, I'm sure. We never left the house that afternoon."

Okay, so maybe Jingles and the boy were somehow communicating, and the cat knew what had happened. He was, after all, a Tansy cat, so anything was possible. I supposed I could ask Finn if the idea of a present could be possible.

"Do you know where the present came from? Who gave it to Santa or put it in the house?"

The boy started to draw again. This time he added a very tall, thin man with a scribbled-out face.

"The man has no face," I said.

Wiley began to rock back and forth and still didn't look directly at me.

"Maybe it was dark. Maybe Wiley saw something thorough his window but couldn't see the man's face because it was dark," Jane suggested.

"Do you think he might have been in the park when the present was placed in the Santa House?" I asked.

"No," Jane answered. "If it was after dark, Wiley would have been in bed. But he does look out his bedroom window, so I suppose he might have seen someone earlier if they walked by. But he has an active imagination, so he might have made the man up."

"Wiley draws often?"

She nodded. "Every day. He draws all sorts of things. Things he sees, but also things that aren't of this world. I figure the monsters and superheroes are images he has picked up from comics or on television. Occasionally, I get the impression he could be drawing something from his dreams. On a few occasions, he's woken up screaming and then motioned for his sketch pad. He's drawn some pretty dark stuff. When he wakes up from a nightmare, drawing seems to help him to process and go back to sleep."

I took a moment to roll this around in my mind. "Are you saying that Wiley's dreams are real?"

The woman pulled back just a bit.

"It's okay if you are." I glanced at the cat. "I talk to cats. Trust me, dreams that are real are not outside my wheelhouse."

After a moment, Jane spoke again. "Sometimes the dreams turn out to be based in reality. Wiley woke up a few months ago and drew a photo of a car filled with people. The car was underwater, and the people were struggling to get out. The next day I heard about the accident on Orcas Island, where a car went into the sea, and all four people in it died."

"I remember that. And Wiley drew the image before you'd heard about the accident?"

She nodded. "He woke up crying and agitated. I gave him his sketch pad, as I always do. The next morning I heard about the accident. Wiley doesn't seem to know about everything that happens. A lot of things he draws never happen, but sometimes it does seem as if his drawings have some connection with reality."

I leaned back in my chair. "Okay. Maybe Wiley is trying to tell us something. Maybe he knows something about what happened at the Santa House that no one else does. Deputy Finnegan is off the island this morning, but I'll talk to him about this when he gets back. I'll call you again this afternoon."

"And the cat?"

I glanced at Jingles. "I think it would be okay if he stayed with Wiley today. If he starts to act all spastic, call me. Like Wiley, Jingles sometimes has a lot to say, but also like Wiley, he has to find creative ways to communicate. For some reason, I've been chosen to interpret for the magical cats that live on the island."

"There are others?"

I nodded. "A lot of others. The cats and I have solved a lot of mysteries, and Jingles and I will solve this one as well."

Chapter 11

The ferry docked minutes before I arrived at the bookstore, so while I would have preferred a few minutes to fill Tara and Cassie in on my interesting morning, I needed to jump right in, making coffee drinks and selling books and novelty items to the throngs of tourists who descended on us. I loved the culture of the bookstore Tara and I had created, but during the busy summer and Christmas seasons, the crowds that we had to deal with often seemed unmanageable.

"Is Willow coming in today?" I asked Tara.

"She is. Noon to five." She glanced toward the clock. "She usually comes in a little early, so she should be here shortly. Can you check the back to see if we have any more peppermint syrup?"

"Yeah, no problem."

"Check for gingerbread syrup too, as long as you're at it."

I was glad we'd come in yesterday to clean and organize everything. The inventory was now neatly unpacked, which made finding both syrups an easy feat, whereas last week, I would have had to begin opening boxes and sorting through things. Once the coffee bar had been restocked, I crossed into the bookstore to help a woman who was looking for a cozy mystery set at Christmastime. We had several good options, so I chatted with her briefly about each one.

By the time Willow arrived, the crowd from the first ferry had dissipated. We'd have a short reprieve until the second ferry of the day docked, and there was a new crowd to deal with.

"I had an interesting morning," I said to Tara, Cassie, and Willow. I shared with them my visit with Jane and Wiley and the telling drawings the boy created, which his mother was sure had first been seen by him in a dream... or in a nightmare.

"So the kid is psychic?" Cassie asked.

I shrugged. "I don't know. All I can say is that he drew the Santa House on fire in one picture, and he made another drawing of the interior of the house, with Santa sitting on a chair, with a present on the floor next to him. He then added fire coming out of the present. I asked him if he knew who had brought the present and he drew a tall, thin man with his face scratched out. I suppose all of it might just exist in his imagination, but the subject matter seemed like a huge coincidence."

"It seems likely the boy does have some sort of psychic ability," Willow agreed. "And from what you've told us, it sounds as if he is connected to the cat in some way."

"I left Jingles with the boy and his mother. I'll pick him up later when I have the chance. I'm hoping that if the cat and the boy spend some time together, they will come up with additional clues that will help Finn track down whoever set the fire at the Santa House."

"Have you spoken to Finn about the drawings yet?" Tara asked.

"No, not yet. He is on San Juan Island today, tracking down a mistletoe vendor. I figure he'll probably be returning to the island on the next ferry. I texted him to let him know that I had news and that he should get in touch with me when he gets back."

Cassie grabbed a rag and began to wipe down the coffee bar while the area was clear. "This mystery seems to have a lot of moving parts, and I still can't decide if everything is connected or not. First Tom died in a fire at the Santa House, and then the island experienced a series of acts of vandalism that on the surface seem as if they could be related but, as it is turning out, aren't necessarily. I mean, what are the odds that the person who shot down the reindeer and the one who set fire to Chappy's Christmas decorations and whoever cut down the tree in the park aren't all the same?"

"I'm not sure about all the acts of vandalism," I said, "but I do know that the reindeer being shot down and the fire on Chappy's boat were isolated incidents."

"I might know something," Tara said. "I'm not sure if it is relevant, but when I was at the bar last night this guy I've seen around town whose name I don't know came in. Danny seemed to know him, so I suppose you can ask him his name. Anyway, the guy told Danny that the safe at the holiday store had been broken into overnight on Sunday, but none of the money was taken. The weird thing was, the entire safe had been filled with mistletoe."

"So someone broke into the store and broke into the safe, but left all the money? Was anything else taken?" I asked.

"The guy who was talking to Danny didn't mention whether anything else was. In fact, the whole conversation ran along the lines of what a fool the vandal was to go to all the trouble of opening the safe and not taking anything."

"The whole thing is bizarre," Cassie agreed. "Every time I hear about the antics of the individual we are referring to as the mistletoe vandal, it makes me think of that Halloween movie we watched as a kid that featured an imp who went around town causing all sorts of trouble. I can't remember the name of the movie, but I do remember that the imp's only intention seemed to be to create chaos wherever he went."

"I remember that movie," I said. "I don't remember the name either, but you're right. Other than the burning of the Santa House, which resulted in a death, the acts committed seem to be focused on causing destruction, but beyond that, there doesn't seem to be any purpose. Maybe Finn will know more when he gets back from San Juan Island. If the mistletoe vendor remembers who he sold the mistletoe tied with green ribbon to, maybe Finn can fill in the rest of the blanks."

"Finn mentioned that in a normal crime spree, the acts committed can escalate in severity," Tara pointed out. "If we take the Santa House out of the equation, that seems to be holding true. We know that on the first night, which would have been last Wednesday, the nativity scene at the church was vandalized and the tree in the park was cut down. Both acts were unfortunate and upset a lot of people, but neither was particularly difficult or risky to accomplish. But then, on the second night of the destruction spree, which took place several days later, the toy store was broken in to, and merchandise was destroyed, and the holiday store was likewise broken in to, and the safe was actually cracked, even if nothing was stolen or trashed. It seems like the mistletoe vandal is upping his game."

"And it's only the seventeenth," Willow pointed out. "How much more damage can this individual inflict if he continues to go on as he's begun?"

Willow was right. If the vandalism continued, and if the severity continued to increase, things could get pretty dicey by the time December 25 rolled around.

Chapter 12

When Finn returned from tracking down the mistletoe vendor with the dark green ribbons, he informed us that, while the man confirmed that most customers purchased only a sprig or two, he had sold a large bag of mistletoe containing thirty sprigs to three college-age men about a week earlier. Finn estimated that between the nativity scene, the tree in the park, the cash register at the toy store, and the safe at the holiday store, about half the sprigs had been recovered. The guys paid the vendor for the bag in cash, so he had no reason to get any of their names. The vendor didn't remember any distinguishing features that would help to identify them, but he did say it seemed as if they all had dark hair. Not a lot to go on, but at least it was something. Finn planned to initiate a search of lodging rentals on the island in the hope of finding the three men that way.

Of course, it was also possible they were staying at a home owned by one of them or a family member.

None of us could understand why three guys hanging out on the island over the holidays would go around vandalizing holiday-themed stores and displays, but perhaps they have some sort of a dare situation going on.

Meanwhile, I told Finn about Wiley and his drawings. I could tell he was intrigued by the notion that the boy might know something about the fire at the Santa House. I assured him I planned to utilize both the boy and the cat in the hope of stumbling on a real clue we could use to bring in the person who'd killed Tom Miller. Finn and I were both of the opinion that if it did turn out that the college-aged men were the individuals vandalizing random shops and displays around town, it was more likely than not that they weren't the ones who had set fire to the Santa House. We both felt that a group of men playing pranks wouldn't start with a big fire that killed a man and then go out that night and chop down a tree and steal a baby Jesus. There was still that small voice in the back of my mind that wouldn't let go of the idea that the random acts of vandalism were nothing more than a decoy to cast suspicion away from whoever had killed Tom Miller, but after seeing Wiley's drawings this morning I was even less convinced that was what had happened.

I decided to leave work early so I could spend a few minutes chatting with Jane while I picked up Jingles. My intuition told me that the key to solving Tom's murder lay in getting to what the cat and the boy knew but would have difficulty communicating. I knew that it was Finn's job to track down the mistletoe vandal, but now that I no longer suspected that the vandal was the one who killed Tom, I was much less interested in him and much more interested in the man, or woman, who'd burned down the Santa House.

"You're early," Jane greeted me when I knocked on her door.

"I hoped that you might have a few minutes to chat. I need to get home to my husband and the baby we are sitting for, so I can't stay long, but the drawings Wiley came up with this morning have been on my mind all day. I think that between them, Wiley and Jingles hold the key to bringing Tom Miller's killer to justice."

"Wiley and Jingles have been up in Wiley's room all day. I know there has been a lot of drawing going on. I didn't want to disturb them because both of them seemed content, but I am willing to try to talk with Wiley to see if he will share his work with us. Just be warned that he may not be."

I nodded. "I wouldn't want to do anything to upset him. Let's just ask him if we can look at his drawings and take it from there."

I followed Jane into Wiley's bedroom. Jingles trotted over to greet me, but Wiley never looked up from the picture he was drawing. There were other pictures scattered all around the room. Some were of the same basic scenes he'd drawn that morning with slight variations. There were additional drawings of Santa in a burning house, additional drawings of a brightly wrapped gift on fire, and other drawings of the interior of the Santa House.

Yet while some of the drawings seemed to be duplicates, others were different. There was a drawing of Santa in a coffin, which I found disturbing, Santa in a boat, which I found less so, and

Santa in a windowless room. On the wall of the room without windows were panels, or perhaps doors.

"What do you make of the drawing of the room?" I asked Jane.

"It feels to me like a cellar. It has a dark feel to it."

I nodded. "I had the same reaction. What do you think is going on with the back wall?"

Jane frowned. "I'm not sure. It seems as if perhaps the wall has doors or drawers built into it. My first thought was that it was a mausoleum, but I'm not so sure."

"Do you think it might be a bank? When I look at the wall, I think of safety deposit boxes."

Jane shrugged. "Maybe. It's hard to tell. The feel of the drawing is dark and almost sinister. But I guess now what you mention it, safety deposit boxes might work as well."

"I guess the main reason it occurred to me that the drawing could be of safety deposit boxes is because we found a key among Tom's possessions. It looked as if it might have belonged to a lockbox of some sort." I paused. "I wonder if Finn ever followed up on that."

"So you think that it's possible whatever is inside a safety deposit box might somehow be related to his death?"

"I don't know. It seems pretty random to me right now, but it might be something to look in to."

I glanced at the other drawings in the room. Among all those duplicates, I also wondered about the ones of the boat. There were quite a few images of Santa in a boat, and while the other drawings felt dark in tone, those did not.

"Do you have a boat, or do you know anyone who does?" I asked.

"No. Wiley has never even ridden in a boat. I did wonder about those drawings. I'm not sure what they're all about."

"I sort of hoped that Wiley might provide additional details about the man with the scribbled-out face, but it seems as if they are all the same."

Jane smiled at her son, who was working on a drawing of a large tree with branches that looked a lot like arms. "If the figure of the man in black is something from his nightmare, he may be blocking out the details of his face. It's so hard to understand why he draws what he does."

Jingles walked over and brushed up against Wiley. He paused what he was doing and looked directly at the cat. The cat butted his head up against the boy's hand, and he smiled.

"Did you see that?" Jane asked.

"See what?"

"Not only did Wiley stop drawing to give his attention to the cat, which he never does, but he smiled, which he also never does."

I put my hand across my heart. "Wow. That is really something. I can see why you want to adopt Jingles so badly."

"In my mind, this cat is the answer to a prayer. Wiley was so upset this morning, but then Jingles showed up and he has been happy and peaceful all day."

There was no way I could take the cat away from this child. "Look, I know I said that I couldn't let you adopt Jingles until we found Tom's killer, but Jingles and Wiley seem to be working together. I can probably leave him here as long as I can come back in the morning to check on things, and as long as you are able to have him overnight."

"I don't have any supplies. Food. A cat box. That sort of thing."

I glanced at the cat, who seemed pretty darn content. "Okay. I'll go get what you need. When I come back, we'll work out a way for Jingles to both work with Wiley and help me find Tom's killer."

"Thank you so much. I can't tell you how much this means to me and Wiley."

I turned to leave the bedroom to get the supplies I'd need to bring back for Jingles from my cabin when one of the drawings caught my eye. "Do you think we could take a closer look at that drawing of the wall of boxes?"

Jane nodded. "Wiley honey, Cait is going to let Jingles stay with you tonight, but she needs to go get some supplies. She would like to look at one of your drawings a little closer. Is that okay?"

The boy reached over and picked up the drawing I wanted to examine and handed it to his mother. He did so without ever looking up from his current drawing.

"Is it okay if I take this?" I asked. "I'll bring it back when I come back with the food and other supplies Jingles will need to stay with you."

He didn't respond. I looked at Jane.

"I think it is okay. If he didn't want you to take it, he would let you know. Let's leave the room and see what happens."

We walked out of the bedroom and down the hallway. Wiley hadn't resisted my taking the drawing that far away, so Jane felt certain he didn't mind my leaving the house with it. I told her I'd be back in an hour and then headed toward my cabin.

Chapter 13

"So what do you make of this?" I showed Cody the drawing Wiley had done as soon as I arrived at my cabin to pick up the things for Jingles.

"It looks like a mausoleum," he answered. "A building where bodies are buried in drawers built into the wall."

"That was my thought as well, but then I wondered if it might be a wall of safety deposit boxes. Finn and I did find a small key among the possessions Tom had in the pocket of the pants he left in his dirty clothes hamper."

"Did Finn ever figure out what the key went to?"

"Not as far as I know," I answered. "I intended to stop by to chat with him, but Tara and I spent the afternoon setting up the cat lounge as a Santa's workshop."

"Won't that be a problem with the cats?" Cody wondered.

"We have no cats for the lounge right now. The ones I had were all adopted, at least the ones we felt were eligible for adoption. I did pick up the new cats this past weekend, but I'm going to wait to take them to the lounge until after the holiday, so the room isn't being used. In the past, we've just set up a chair for Alex in the bookstore, but he is such a popular Santa, there is always a line to see him, so we figured there would be more space if we used the cat lounge. You should see the place. Tara got a lot of new decorations. It looks adorable."

"I'll stop by tomorrow. Maybe I'll bring Sammy."

I glanced at the infant, who was watching us from his bouncy chair. "We did talk about getting a photo of him with Santa for his parents. I guess that would be as good a time as any." I began gathering the supplies. "I'm going to run this stuff over to Jane, but then I'll be right back. Do you want me to pick up some food?"

"I guess that might be a good idea. I never did make it to the market."

"How about Mexican?"

"Sounds good."

"Maybe I'll call Siobhan to see if they want to join us if they haven't eaten yet. She was busy with two babies today, so she might be happy not to have to cook."

As it turned out, Siobhan was thrilled with the idea of not having to cook, so I explained that I had to drop off the cat stuff and pick up the food and then Cody and Sammy and I would be over.

******

"So, did you find the college-aged guys who bought the mistletoe?" I asked Finn once we'd each served ourselves from the selection of enchiladas, tacos, tamales, and beans and rice I'd brought.

"I did. As I expected, they'd rented a house on the island. When I first spoke to them, they denied having been responsible for the vandalism, but when I brought up the fact that a man had died in the fire at the Santa House and someone was going down for murder, they confessed to the lesser crimes. They are in jail on San Juan Island now, but I'm sure they'll be processed and then released, but I can guarantee you when they get the bill for the damage they caused, they are going to wish they'd found a less expensive way to pledge a club."

"Is that why they did it?" I asked. "They were pledging a club?"

"That's what they said," Finn confirmed.

"And you are sure they aren't also responsible for the Santa House?" Siobhan asked.

"I don't believe they had anything to do with that. The other crimes were petty in nature, and the fire at the Santa House feels like it was set by someone with knowledge about arson. The men I spoke to were just a bunch of goofy kids who got together and made a lot of really bad decisions during their Christmas break from college."

"Well, I'm glad we have at least part of the crime spree solved," I said. "Now we can focus on the Santa House. Did you look at the copy of the drawing I left for you?"

Finn nodded. "It has a familiar feel to it, but I can't say that I know offhand where a wall with boxes might be."

"I thought they might be safety deposit boxes. Did you find a safety deposit box to go with the key?"

"No. I checked all the banks on the island, and the key is not a match for any of their systems. I figure the key either goes to something else entirely, or it belongs to a safety deposit box located off the island."

"I guess we should refocus on the individuals with a motive to want Tom dead," I said. "I feel like there have been so many distractions, we may have lost focus, which, again, is something Tansy warned me about."

"I still can't believe that none of the other acts of vandalism ended up being connected to the fire at the Santa House," Cody said. "I mean really, what are the odds that we'd have so many incidents, all relating to Christmas in some way, and yet not have them connect to one another?"

"It seems unlikely," I agreed. "Yet that does seem to be the case."

We fell silent as we ate our dinner. Afterward, Cody and Finn got up to see to the dishes, leaving Siobhan and me alone.

"Are you still able to watch Sammy tomorrow evening while Cody and I are at play rehearsal?" I asked her.

"Yeah, we can watch him. How is the play coming along?"

I groaned. "Let's just say it will take a real Christmas miracle for us to pull it off this year. Cody and I haven't been able to do extra rehearsals, as we have in the past, and I feel like the kids are distracted. I'm glad we decided on a small production at the church rather than the larger one we sometimes hold at the community center. I figure most of the audience will be parents and other family members, so maybe they'll be more forgiving if all the kids haven't learned their lines."

"Did you remind them to practice at home?"

"I did. That doesn't mean they did, however."

"If you can get the kids to come for an extra rehearsal, I can watch Sammy," Siobhan volunteered.

"I was thinking about doing one on Friday. I guess we'll see how tomorrow's rehearsal goes. I feel like it isn't just the kids who have been distracted. Between having Sammy to take care of and moving and the remodel, I feel like Cody and I are on overload most of the time."

"Just another week and it will all be over one way or another," Siobhan said.

I knew she was trying to be encouraging, but the reminder that Christmas was less than ten days away did not leave me feeling more confident at all.

"Do you need help with the Christmas Eve party?" Siobhan asked.

"Francine is doing the turkeys again," I said, referring to our next-door neighbor. "You and Tara are already taking care of most of the side dishes. Cody and I plan to decorate the ballroom as soon as we finish moving our stuff out of there. Danny ordered the wine, and Mom is going to make a nonalcoholic punch. I think we have everything covered as long as everything else in our lives goes smoothly between now and then."

"Mr. Parsons is so grateful for all you do for him that I don't think he is going to care a bit if everything isn't perfect," Siobhan reminded me. "How many guests have you confirmed?"

"Around eighty-five," I answered. "But there always end up being additional folks with nowhere to go for Christmas Eve, so we are planning for a hundred."

"Just let us know what you need," Siobhan said. "Finn and I want to help. Don't we?" she asked as Finn and Cody wandered back into the room.

"As long as I don't have to work," Finn replied.

I frowned. I supposed that if we hadn't identified Tom's killer by Christmas, Finn might not end up being able to take a few days off as he'd hoped. We had another week to figure this out. We'd just need to step up our game.

Chapter 14

Wednesday, December 18

Wiley's mom called me the first thing that morning. She shared that while Wiley and Jingles had gotten along fabulously the previous evening, Wiley had awoken early today from what appeared to have been a bad dream. He had been drawing frantically ever since, and the cat seemed restless as well. She wondered if I could stop by on my way to work. She wasn't sure if I should take the cat home with me for a while or if it would be better to leave him with Wiley, but I had asked her to call me if the cat started acting oddly and in her mind the way he'd been behaving this morning definitely qualified as strange.

I called Tara and filled her in. Cody had already planned to take Sammy to day care, and he offered to take Max into the newspaper with him, so he was covered as well. I grabbed a cup of coffee and a piece of toast and headed out the door a full thirty minutes earlier than I would have otherwise. I figured even with the early start, by the time I drove to Harthaven, sussed out the situation, and got back to Coffee Cat Books, I'd wind up being late. I really wanted to be on time because today was Alex's first day as Santa, but all I could do was all I could do.

Jane met me at the door. The poor woman looked exhausted. I offered her my most encouraging smile and tried to assure her that I was certain that everything would be okay. When I walked into Wiley's bedroom, Jingles ran straight over to me despite the dozens and dozens of drawings on the floor.

"Wow. Someone has been busy." I bent over to pick up the cat.

Wiley didn't look in my direction, but I hadn't expected him to. There were a lot of drawings of the man with no face, but there were also a lot of Santa sitting on a chair with a brightly wrapped gift beside him. In a few of the drawings, fire was coming out of the top of the package. The drawings were similar to those he'd drawn of the Santa House the day before, but the ribbon on the package was green this time rather than red, and the seat in which Santa sat was less of a throne and more of a plush chair.

I supposed that just because the details between yesterday's drawings and today's were slightly different didn't necessarily mean they were significant, but still, they did seem worth noting.

"Meow," Jingles said, struggling to get down.

I set him on the floor. He headed for the door.

I glanced at Jane. "It looks like he might want to go with me."

She glanced at the cat. "It does look that way. Does he always tell you what he wants in this way?"

"Usually. He paws at stuff, knocks stuff onto the floor, scratches at the door, and meows incessantly when he wants to get my attention."

Jane smiled. "A lot like Wiley. Will you bring him back when you are done doing whatever it is he wants you to do?"

I nodded. "Sure. I can do that."

Jane looked at Wiley, who was still drawing. "Jingles is going to go with Cait for a while, but he'll be back."

Wiley picked up one of his drawings and held it out. He didn't look up, but I sensed he wanted me to have it, so I reached out to take it. He went back to drawing, and I looked at the paper. Santa was in his chair, a brightly wrapped package with flames coming out of it next to him, and a tall man with no face stood in the background. This drawing also had a cat in it that looked a lot like Jingles. The cat was clawing at Santa's leg.

"Thank you, Wiley," I said. "As soon as Jingles and I take care of whatever he wants me to do, I will bring him back."

Jingles was restless on the way to the bookstore. When we arrived, he went straight in. Alex was already there, dressed in his Santa suit, despite the fact that his shift didn't begin for another half hour. There was a short line at the coffee bar, so once I'd let Jingles into the cat lounge, I went to help Tara. Cassie was off today, but Willow was scheduled to help Santa when the kids began to arrive. As long as none of us were pulled away, we should have things covered.

When the customers at the coffee bar left, I headed to the cat lounge to see how Alex was doing. I glanced into the room to see Alex sitting in his chair with a brightly wrapped gift next to him. Jingles was clawing at his leg, but Alex was ignoring him.

"Did you add that present after we finished decorating yesterday?" I asked Tara about the gift with the bright green ribbon.

"No. I noticed it this morning but thought that maybe you put it there. It does seem to round things out nicely."

"Alex," I yelled, "get out of there." I looked around the bookstore. "Everyone out. Now!"

I imagine it was the panic in my voice that demanded to be heard, because as soon as I started yelling, every single person in the bookstore, including Alex, piled out onto the wharf. I looked around for the two women at the coffee bar, the blond-haired man with the green sweater, the red-headed woman with the two children who looked to be under ten, and the preteens who'd been giggling in the back of the store near the romance books. It looked as if everyone had made it out. I did one final sweep of the crowd and then panic set in.

"What is it?" Tara asked.

"Did you see Jingles?" I demanded.

"He's there." Tara pointed to the front door as he trotted out.

I pulled out my phone and called Finn. "I think there is a bomb in the…"

My call was interrupted by a loud bang.

"Oh God," Tara said as the cat lounge became engulfed in flames.

Chapter 15

Finn heard the explosion through the phone and responded immediately. The fire department arrived quickly, and the damage from the fire seemed to be contained in the cat lounge. Thanks to Wiley's drawing, I was able to get everyone out in time, so there were no human or feline casualties. Of course, the damage was such that the store was going to be closed for months and months for repairs. Luckily, we had insurance for both the structure and the contents because, by the time the fire was out, the books and novelties in inventory were completely destroyed.

Tara and I were in shock over the loss of our business, but we were both so happy that no one had gotten hurt that we found ourselves relieved rather than traumatized. We would just have to handle each moment as it came. We'd deal with the cleanup and the paperwork right off the bat, and once the insurance claim was settled, we'd rebuild and start again.

"I have to say that it is amazing that Wiley knew what was going to happen before it did," Siobhan said when she came by the scene of the fire to offer comfort. "And I am so incredibly grateful to him for providing a warning. Buildings can be replaced. People can't."

I couldn't agree more. My heart must have stopped and started a dozen times in the past couple of hours. First, it stopped when I saw the scene Wiley drew for me play out before my eyes. Then it started once again in that split second when I was sure everyone had made it out safely. It stopped yet again when the building blew, only to start beating when Finn and the fire team arrived. All in all, it had been a horrific day, and I was sure the real shock would set in later, but, as Siobhan had said, buildings could be replaced and no one was hurt. For that, I'd be eternally grateful.

My car, as well as Tara's, had been parked in front of the store and was blocked in by the firetrucks. Cody had shown up shortly after the blast, so I'd put Jingles inside it with Max. Now that the fire was out and the crowd had begun to dissipate, I felt my knees begin to wobble just a bit as shock set in, but I took a deep breath and forced myself to focus on the tasks at hand.

"The maniac who did this could have killed a lot of people today," I said to Cody. "That's two Santas in two weeks. He has to be stopped."

"I agree. What do you want to do now?"

"I want to take Jingles back to Wiley, as I promised I would. I want to try to thank him for his part in saving the lives of everyone inside the bookstore. I don't know if he'll understand me, but I need to try. I want to look at all his drawings once again to see what else he may be trying to tell me. And then I want to get the Scooby Gang together to really flesh this out. Now that the mistletoe vandal distraction has been put to bed, maybe we can focus on the Santa killer better than we were able to the last time we met."

"What about rehearsal?" Cody asked.

I closed my eyes and groaned. "I totally forgot about that."

"Maybe Sister Mary can cover for us," Cody said. "She helps out with the play every year. She knows what to do."

"Okay," I said. "You call her. I'll tell the others what we'd like to do."

The others agreed to meet at Finn and Siobhan's place later in the evening. There was room upstairs to put both Connor and Sammy to bed, and plenty of space for the rest of us to meet and share a meal. Finn had to take care of the paperwork relating to the fire, and Cody and I would be going by to see Wiley, so Tara and Danny offered to get the food and drinks for everyone while Siobhan picked up both babies from day care, took them home, and got them fed, bathed, and ready for bed. Cassie was on San Juan Island today, but as soon as I called her and explained what had happened, she assured me she'd be home by the time we all met.

Cody and I moved my car to the newspaper office, deciding to leave it there overnight. Siobhan had taken Max with her, so we drove to Harthaven in Cody's vehicle with Jingles, who I was seriously going to treat with a giant piece of salmon when this was over. I still wasn't sure how the timing had come together the way it had. Wiley must have seen the event in his mind before it occurred, knowing that the cat would be clawing at Alex's leg at the exact moment I happened to look into the cat lounge.

"Cait." Jane opened the door just as I knocked, stepped out onto the stoop, and gave me a long, hard hug. "I heard what happened. I was so worried."

"I'm fine." I hugged her back. "Thanks to Wiley and Jingles. If not for the drawing Wiley gave me, I would never have known to get everyone out of the store."

Jane gave me one more hard squeeze and then stepped back. "My son really is exceptional. Sometimes I forget that. Sometimes I get tired and overwhelmed and only focus on the negative, and then something like this happens, and I realize that Wiley is exactly who he is supposed to be." She took a step back. "Come on in. Both of you," she added as she noticed Cody.

He stepped into the entry and sct Jingles down on the floor. The cat ran up the stairs.

"I'd like to thank Wiley for saving my life and the lives of a whole lot of other people," I said. "I realize he may not acknowledge my presence, but I really need to tell him what an amazing thing he did today."

"He can hear you and understand what you are saying," Jane answered. "He may not look at you or respond in any way, but he'll know what is in your heart."

Jane started up the stairs, I fell in behind her, and Cody followed. When we arrived at Wiley's bedroom, the boy and the cat were looking into each other's eyes.

"Cait is here," Jane said. "And she brought her husband. She wants to talk to you."

Wiley didn't look directly at me, but he turned slightly so he was facing me a bit more. I supposed that was something.

"I wanted to let you know that your drawing saved my life today," I said in a gentle voice. "And not just my life, but the lives of some of my friends and customers. I owe you more than I can ever say, but for now, I just want to thank you. You are an amazing person."

"And I want to thank you as well," Cody added. "I can't imagine my life without my wife. I owe you so much for finding a way to warn her."

"I know you and Jingles would like to spend some time together now," I jumped back in, "so I will leave him here again tonight, but before I go, is there anything else I need to know?"

The boy picked up a drawing. He held it in my direction. I glanced at Jane. She nodded. I took a step forward and accepted the paper. I thanked Wiley once again, and then Jane, Cody, and I went back downstairs.

"What's the drawing of?" Cody asked.

I looked at it and then turned it around so he could see what Wiley had drawn.

"What do you think he is trying to tell you?" Cody asked.

"I have no idea."

Chapter 16

We left Jane's place, and Cody and I headed back to the peninsula. I realized as we made the trip that due to circumstances was beyond my control, I'd done nothing to keep my promise to Cassie to go through my stuff and be out of my cabin by the end of the week. I supposed that finding the maniac who seemed to be bent on destruction was a lot more important, and I was sure she'd understand, but I could remember my excitement at getting my own place for the very first time and understood why she might be showing signs of impatience. Still, I felt bad that I was making her wait. Cody had moved almost everything that had to go; all I really needed to do was make one final walkthrough to make sure I had everything I wanted to take. Then I could turn the keys over to Cassie, and we could both get on to the next phases of our lives.

"Did Sammy go down okay?" I asked Siobhan when we arrived at the home she shared with Finn and Connor. Cody had stopped over at the cabin to feed Max and make sure he was settled in for a few hours before heading to the big house for the meeting.

"He was a total angel. He ate his dinner, smiled through his bath, and went right to sleep when I put him down."

I couldn't help but roll my eyes because I'd never had even one bedtime ritual go half as smoothly as Siobhan described. I might as well admit if only to myself, that babies and I weren't a good mix.

"Conner went down easily as well," Siobhan added. "Once everyone gets here, we should be all set to dig right in."

"Do you know when Finn will be here?" I asked.

"Soon. Danny texted; he and Tara will be here in about five minutes, and Cassie is about five minutes behind them. So, what did Wiley have to say?"

I showed her the drawing.

"What do you think this means?"

I slowly shook my head. "I'm not sure."

The drawing showed Santa sitting on a chair with a young child with blond hair in his lap. A woman was standing in front of Santa, also with blond hair, and a tall man dressed all in black with a scratched-out face was standing behind her. He seemed to be reaching for her in a menacing way.

"The feel of the drawing is that of a mother in danger from the man in black," Siobhan said. "You don't think this is Wiley's mother and the child is him?"

"Jane didn't think it was her. The woman in the drawing has long blond hair, and Jane has short brown hair. She also pointed out that if the image was of her, Wiley would have been frantic, and he wasn't.

I asked for a clue, and he handed me the drawing, but he wasn't agitated and upset like he was this morning when I was there and he showed me the drawing that led to my clearing out the bookstore before it blew up. If I had to guess, this drawing is of something that either happened in the past or may happen in the future but isn't imminent."

"If this is a prophecy of some sort, let's hope it never happens at all." Siobhan swallowed hard. "I can almost picture the woman dead on the floor."

I looked at Siobhan. "You have long blond hair, and the child could be Connor."

Siobhan frowned. "You think?"

I shrugged. "There are a lot of women in the world with long blond hair."

I could see that Siobhan was concerned when she handed the drawing back to me. Maybe I shouldn't have pointed out the similarities between the drawing and her and Connor, but I also felt it was better to be prepared than to find yourself in a situation you never saw coming.

By the time Siobhan and I had made our way to the kitchen, Danny and Tara had shown up with the food. I grabbed some plates and utensils while Siobhan went for the glasses and napkins. Just as we had everything set out, Cody arrived from next door, and Cassie arrived from the ferry. When Finn pulled into the drive, we took the covers off the food, and everyone began to serve themselves.

"The food looks wonderful," I said to Tara. "You must have read my mind when you decided on Italian."

"It sounded good, and I feel like we've had a lot of pizza lately. I got the usual spaghetti and meatballs and fettuccine Alfredo, but I also got some of the daily special, penne pasta with spicy sausage in a creamy chipotle sauce."

"That sounds wonderful. I'll have to try it."

"How was Wiley when you stopped by?" Tara asked.

"He was drawing, as he has been every time I've seen him. This time, though, he handed me a disturbing drawing of a mother and child visiting Santa, with the man with the scratched-out face lurking behind the woman."

"Do you think the drawing is a warning?"

I pursed my lips. "I'm not sure. This morning he was really agitated when he showed me the drawing about what was going to happen at the bookstore, but he handed me this one when I asked if he had any clues he wanted to pass along to me. My gut tells me the drawing is of something either in the past or in the very distant future. It seems if anyone was in immediate danger, he would have been a lot more animated than he was."

"Still, we might want to keep our eyes and ears open," Tara pointed out.

"I couldn't agree more."

Tara and I joined the others at the table. Once we'd eaten, Finn began to speak immediately. A lot had happened in the past few hours; I was sure he had a lot of data to disseminate to us.

"First, I just want to say that I am very grateful that we are all here this evening to have this meeting. Things could have turned out a lot more tragically than they did."

Everyone agreed with Finn's assessment of the situation.

"Before we jump into the discussion of the attack on Santa at Coffee Cat Books, which I realize is the real reason we're here, I want to share a few things I found out about Tom and the things we found in his pocket when Jingles led Cait to his home."

Everyone sat quietly, waiting for Finn to continue.

"As you remember, Cait and I found a key, four quarters, a phone number, and a bullet casing in the pockets of a pair of pants Tom had left in his dirty clothes basket. We aren't certain any of these items are connected to what happened to him, but the cat led Cait to the house and seemed satisfied when we'd found it, so we assumed the items in Tom's pockets were what we were there to find. I've spent some time looking closely at all the items. Initially, we felt that the key might be associated with a safety deposit box because it was smaller than the sort of key one might have for a house or automobile, but I checked all the banks on the island and was unable to find a match. Quite by accident, I stumbled onto some information while at the Driftwood for an early breakfast this morning. It seems that Tom purchased a boat a couple of weeks ago. It is docked at the private marina on the north shore, and it was not widely known that he'd bought it. In fact, he hadn't even gotten around to registering it in his name yet. The man from whom I got the information about the boat was a buddy of Tom's. He stopped by my table to see if I had any leads on his death. We got to chatting, and he not only told me about the boat but also where to find it. As soon as I finished eating, I headed to the old marina to check it out. The boat is a cabin cruiser, and below deck, I found a wall with cabinets that lock. The key Cait and I found opens them."

"Wiley drew Santa on a boat," I said.

"I thought of that as soon as I found out that Tom had bought a boat," Finn replied. "And when I saw the wall of cabinets we thought might have been either a mausoleum or safety deposit boxes, I realized this was what Wiley had actually drawn."

"So what is in the cabinets?" Siobhan asked.

"A variety of things, the most interesting of which was a bag of Washington quarters like the ones we found in Tom's pocket."

I narrowed my gaze. "Okay, so why did Tom have all those quarters? I thought you said they weren't all that valuable."

"Generally speaking that is true, but coins, if uncirculated, which these appear to be, can bring in a pretty penny. I suppose that the coins would hold a certain appeal for a collector. But then I noticed that again, as with the four we found in a pocket, all the coins in the bag are dated between 1932, which is the first year they were circulated, and 1935. I still don't know why Tom had the coins, but given the fact that they were uncirculated, I figured they came from a collector. After doing some research into the history of the coin, though, I found that there were no Washington quarters minted in 1933 at any US mint."

"What are you saying?" Danny asked.

"I think the coins are fake. They look real to me, and I'm not sure why anyone would go to all the trouble to counterfeit them, but that is the only explanation I can come up with. I've already sent a few of the coins off to someone who knows a lot more about this sort of thing than I do."

The room fell into silence, everyone probably trying to make sense of the information Finn had just shared.

"What could any of this have to do with Tom's death?" Tara asked.

Finn shrugged. "Maybe nothing. I can't explain why Tom bought a boat or had possession of what I think are counterfeit Washington quarters, but both appear to be true. In addition to the bag of quarters I found in one locked cabinet, there were also some old letters and journals, several old maps, a sextant, a compass, and a few other items that would suggest he planned to go somewhere, perhaps to look for something. I haven't had a chance to read the letters or journals yet. Hopefully, they will provide some insight into what Tom was up to."

"Any guess as to what it might have been?" Cassie asked.

"If you remove the quarters from the equation, I would say he was planning to head off on a quest, or perhaps a treasure hunt. It's hard to know at this point. What I will say is that Wiley drew both Santa in a boat and a wall of locked cabinets on the boat. That says to me that Tom actually is part of whatever is going on, not just someone who happened to be playing Santa when someone blew up the Santa House."

"If Tom himself was the intended victim, as opposed to Santa or the Santa House itself being the intended victim, how does Alex and Coffee Cat Books fit into this?" I asked.

"I don't know," Finn answered. "It just seems to me that if we weren't supposed to look at Tom as an individual in addition to his role as Santa, Cait's cat wouldn't have led her to his house so that we would find those items, and Wiley wouldn't have drawn Santa on a boat and the wall of cabinets."

No one disputed Finn's logic. Still we were attempting to assign motive to the actions of a cat and an autistic child. The reality was there most likely wasn't a way to know for certain why either had done what they had.

"Maybe whoever killed Tom realized that a second attack on an island Santa would get Finn to look for someone with a grudge against Santa rather than a grudge against Tom," I said.

"I suppose that might be possible," Finn said. "To be safe, perhaps we should do what we did during our first meeting and put together two lists: people who might want Tom dead and people who might want Santa dead."

"We came up with Clifford Little and Wilson Tyson before as people with good reasons to hate Christmas," I reminded the group. "If you remember, Clifford's wife and son died in a house fire started by a Christmas tree, and Wilson's wife died in a car accident two days before Christmas last year."

"I spoke to both of them," Finn said, "and while it is true that neither of them is looking forward to the holiday, I didn't sense that either had taken out their pain on the island's Santas. I do think that looking at others who might share this same sort of pain is a good idea. I can't imagine having to deal with such a significant loss and also having it coincide with the time of the year that is supposed to bring joy and good tidings."

"What about Alton Peyton?" Danny asked. "He didn't suffer a death, but his wife left him on

Christmas Eve last year. The poor guy was pretty destroyed when she left town not only with most of their joint savings but also his best friend. He was in the bar last week, and it seemed obvious he was still pretty mad about the whole thing."

"I suppose that anger is as good a motivator as deeply felt grief," Finn said. "I'll talk to him."

"If you think Tom's killer could be female, you might want to add Nancy Morton to your list of people to talk to," Tara said. "Nancy hates Christmas. I'm not sure why, but ever since I've known her, once Thanksgiving rolls around, she starts to complain about every carol on the radio, every decoration in town, and every event on the island."

"Okay. I'll add her as well. Anyone else?"

We continued to discuss all the local Grinches before we moved on to people with grudges against Tom, just in case the explosion at the bookstore was a decoy and Tom was the victim after all.

"Last time we discussed Tom's brother-in-law, Darby Weston, and his ex-employee, Gil Errington," Finn said. "I spoke to both. Darby still thinks that I should formally investigate Tom's part in the death of his sister even though Tom is dead, but he seemed more interested in wanting to prove Tom's guilt than anything and was actually angry that he's dead, because it meant he would never be able to get the guy to confess that he'd contributed to his wife's death. I don't think he is our guy. Gil, on the other hand, seemed to feel that Tom got what he deserved. I picked up more of a revenge vibe from him, which might suggest he had a part in Tom's death. He seems to have an alibi, but because we don't know exactly when the timer and ignition spark were set up in the

Santa House, an alibi for the day of the explosion only goes so far. I plan to keep an eye on him."

"What about someone associated with whatever Tom was doing with the boat and the quarters?" I asked.

Finn nodded. "That is a possibility as well."

We came up with a couple more names before Siobhan said, "I think that in addition to suspects, we should discuss other potential victims if it turns out that Santa, and not Tom, is the target. Now that we've had a second incident it does appear likely that it is actually Santa our arsonist is after."

Finn nodded toward his wife. "I agree."

Siobhan continued. "I've been thinking about the situation, and as far as I know, the only other Santa on the island is the one who is scheduled to listen to children's wishes this weekend during the Christmas on the Island event."

"The toy store had a Santa on the weekends," Cassie informed us. "I'm assuming they will have things cleaned up and be open again by the weekend. I don't know for certain they will bring Santa back, but they might."

"And the library usually has a Santa during the little party they throw the Saturday before Christmas," Tara added.

"Okay, so that is three potential victims." Finn jotted down some notes.

"Unless we catch this guy before the weekend, I think we might want to require everyone on the island to forgo having a Santa this year," Cody suggested. "I know that isn't fair to the businesses or the children, but there are too many unknowns at this point for us to simply decide that the person who blew up the Santa House and the bookstore won't strike again."

"I'm not sure we can require anyone to do or not do anything without the island council meeting and coming up with some sort of official declaration," Siobhan pointed out. "And trust me, that is not going to happen before the weekend. But that doesn't mean we can't spread the word to make folks aware of what is going on. It never hurts to ask for voluntary cooperation."

"I agree," Finn said. "We need to spread the word to make sure that everyone is aware of what has already occurred and the sort of danger they might be putting themselves in if they do insist on going ahead with a Santa this year."

The group fell silent. Eventually, Tara spoke. "This is just so overwhelming. How is Finn supposed to know how to best proceed when we can't even decide if it was Tom or Santa who was the target when the Santa House burned down? I've been sitting here listening as the conversation seems to be centered around Tom at one moment and Santa the next."

Cassie picked up the drawing Wiley had given me that afternoon. "We might not know with any certainty if the two explosions are a campaign against Santa or an elaborate scheme to eliminate Tom, but we seem to have someone who knows what is going to happen before it occurs. Maybe we should spend some time really analyzing this."

"I'm not sure this drawing is urgent like the one Wiley gave me this morning, but it can't hurt to discuss it," I agreed. "The images could be literal, but they might also be symbolic."

"Symbolic how?" Tara asked.

I lifted a shoulder. "I don't know. Maybe Wiley is channeling the killer, who is angry at Santa for the death of something or someone close to his heart. It could be the death of a person, but it could also be the death of a childhood belief or even childhood innocence. We said before that people deal with loss in different ways. It is so hard to know what might send a person over the edge. The death of a loved one seems the most likely, but I don't suppose that is the only explanation."

"Maybe we should focus on the box in the bookstore," Finn said. "How did it get there? If neither Cait nor Tara put it there, someone had access to the cat lounge. Maybe if we can figure out who was in there and when the package first showed up, we can figure out how it might have gotten there."

"It wasn't there when we decorated yesterday," I said.

Finn looked at Tara. "When did you notice it?"

"Not until after Alex arrived. When I first got to the store this morning, I was busy stocking the coffee bar and straightening the shelves. We didn't have any cats today, so there was no reason to go into the cat lounge. Alex showed up about an hour before he was due to start his shift. He used the storage room to get dressed. Once he was ready, we both walked into the cat lounge to make sure everything was ready for Santa. I noticed the gift but really didn't think anything of it. I guess after what happened at the Santa House I should have been concerned about the addition of a gift, but I just assumed that Cait had stopped by at some point and set it next to the Santa chair. When I arrived at the bookstore this morning, the place was locked up tight. There was no evidence of forced entry, and nothing was disturbed."

"So how did the person who left the box get in?" Cassie asked.

"After you arrived to stock the shelves and whatnot, did you lock the door behind you?" Finn asked.

"No," Tara admitted. "I just came in and started getting the store ready. I was expecting a delivery and wanted the delivery guy to be able to get in okay, and at that point, I figured Cait would be arriving right behind me. I also knew Alex planned to come in early; I just wasn't sure how early. As it turned out, I was at the store by myself for quite a while before anyone else showed up, but once I started working, I got busy, and it never occurred to me to lock the door."

"Did anyone come in prior to the store opening?" Finn asked.

"I arrived at around eight-thirty. Maeve Portman dropped off baked goods to sell in the coffee bar like she does every morning at around nine." Maeve owned a bakery in town. Originally, Tara had taken care of baking the muffins and scones we sold along with the coffee drinks, but we soon realized that all that baking would be too time-consuming, so we began purchasing them from bakeries and then reselling them. "The cargo ferry arrived at nine-thirty and Phil dropped off the delivery I was expecting." Phil Colton was in charge of delivering the packages that were sent to the island via ferry. "I opened at ten, and a lot of folks were in and out after that. I was there alone, so it is possible that someone could have slipped into the lounge and left the package while I was working the coffee bar without my noticing it."

"What time did you notice the package?" Finn asked.

"I guess around eleven. Alex showed up at around ten-thirty. He happened to show up during a lull, so I walked him into the backroom to show him where he could change. I was only in the back for a few minutes, and when I came back into the main room, it was still empty. So, it would have been around eleven when Alex and I walked into the cat lounge to check things out, and that was when I noticed the package. Cait arrived shortly after that. There was a short line, so she helped me with the coffee bar. I'm not sure what Alex was doing at that point."

"Is that how you remember it?" Finn asked me.

I nodded. "When I arrived Alex, was already there and dressed. As Tara said, I went to help her because there was a line at the coffee bar. By the time customers were taken care of, it was close to time for Santa to begin seeing kids. I guess it was around eleven-thirty then, and we'd been advertising that Santa would be there beginning at noon. I headed to the cat lounge to check on Alex, and that was when I saw the scene Wiley had drawn and got everyone out."

"So the bomb was set to go off before the kids would have begun to line up?" Finn asked.

"Yes. Maybe thirty minutes before," I answered. "Maybe less. At least twenty. Theoretically, one could suggest that the person who set the bomb didn't intend to hurt anyone. If Alex hadn't shown up early, no one would have been in the cat lounge at the time of the explosion. Similarly, the bomb in the Santa

House went off an hour before it was set to open. Still, the bomber must not have been too concerned about human casualties to cut it so close. If all they really wanted to do was blow up a building, they could have done that in the middle of the night when no one at all would be around."

Finn blew out a long, slow breath. I could sense that he was disturbed by the sequence of events. It was odd that someone had been able to plant the package without having broken in during the overnight hours, but if someone did break in, they were able to do so in such a manner as to leave no evidence behind.

"Who has keys to the store?" Finn asked.

Tara answered. "Cait and I, of course. Cassie and Willow." She paused. "And Phil."

"Phil?" Finn asked.

"He takes care of sorting and delivering the packages that arrive on the ferry to the merchants on the island. Today, he came by when I was there, but sometimes he needs to drop items off for us before we open or on days we are closed. I trust him," Tara defended herself. "He's been doing that job for years. A lot of folks prefer to pick up their inventory at the ferry themselves rather than trust Phil with a key, but he knows where to stack the things he drops off for us, and it just seems easier to allow him to come in than it would be for Cait or me to haul everything across the wharf ourselves."

"Phil wouldn't blow up Santa," I said. "You've met him. He's a nice guy who has been doing this job for a long time."

"I don't think Phil blew up Coffee Cat Books, but the odds are that he doesn't keep the key on his body.

It is probably stored, along with the keys of other shops with whom he has the same arrangement, somewhere in the ferry office."

Tara frowned. "I guess I didn't think of that."

"I'll have a chat with Phil tomorrow. Maybe he knows who else might have access to those keys."

Chapter 17

Thursday, December 19

By the following morning, the reality of what had happened had slammed into me. I'm not sure why I hadn't been more upset the day before. The business Tara and I had poured ourselves into was gone. Okay, maybe it wasn't gone. It could and would be repaired, but we had suffered a huge setback. I supposed that I was still in shock after the explosion. I remember going to visit Wiley and Jane and then coming back for the meeting. I didn't remember feeling like I wanted to melt into a puddle of tears, but that was exactly the way it was this morning.

My thoughts turned to Tara. This must be even worse for her. While the bookstore had been both our dreams, it was Tara who had really pulled it all together. I picked up my phone. There were four missed calls, all from Tara.

"I'm sorry," I said as soon as she answered. "I just looked at my phone."

"I don't know what to do." The fact that she'd been crying was evident in her voice. "I woke up early, and my first thought was that I needed to go in early to restock the shelves. And then I remembered. I feel so lost."

"I know. Come over. We'll figure this out together."

She paused and then answered. "Okay. Thanks. I would like that. I'll be there in about an hour."

I hung up and looked around the room. I could hear Cody and Sammy downstairs. I could also smell coffee and bacon. It was time to get up to face whatever it was that this day would bring.

"Coffee?" Cody asked as I walked into the room.

"Please." I accepted the mug and then sat down at the table. "Sammy looks like he has more of his breakfast down the front of him than he managed to get inside."

"It was a challenge this morning," Cody admitted. "Do you want some breakfast?"

"Not yet. Tara is coming over so we can figure out what we need to do about the bookstore. I'm going to have my coffee and then run up to take a shower."

"How's she holding up?" Cody asked.

"Not well."

Cody put a hand on mine. "How are you holding up?"

"About the same." I smiled at my wonderful husband. "But I have you and Sammy, so at least I'm not alone to deal with my emotions. It'll be better if Tara hangs out with us today."

Cody got up, grabbed the pot, and refilled my coffee.

"Are you going into the paper?" I asked.

"I should. For a while. But if you need me, I'll work something out."

I shook my head. "No. I'm fine. You go ahead and do what you need to. I might work on finishing up my packing. I did indicate to Cassie that she could move in here by the end of the week and I'd like to keep that promise. And I need to go get my car."

"Finn brought it over. It's in the drive. Do you want me to take Sammy to day care?" Cody asked.

"That might be best. I will probably head into town to check in with Finn later. I want to check in with Jane, Wiley, and Jingles as well. I think I'll ask Tara to come with me. It will help her keep her mind off things." I took a sip of my coffee. "I wonder if we need to call someone. Like the insurance company. Knowing Tara, though, she is on top of that. I'll just ask her when she gets here."

"If you need help with any of this, you only need to ask," Cody said.

I smiled at him. "I know. And I will."

Suddenly, it felt like the weight of the world was on my shoulders.

"I spoke to Sister Mary this morning," Cody said after a moment. "She said the rehearsal last night went fine. She offered to take over the lead to free us up. She understands that with everything that is going on, our attention will be divided."

"That's nice of her, and to be honest, I'm inclined to take her up on her offer."

"Me too," Cody agreed. "I did tell her that I'd talk to you and call her back, which I will do while you take your shower."

I glanced out the window at the snow flurries in the air. A bit of snow would be nice, but a lot of snow… I wasn't sure I could deal with that on top of everything else right now.

******

By the time I'd showered and dressed, Tara had arrived, and Cody had left with Sammy. I wasn't sure what to say to her, so I simply opened my arms and hugged her while she cried. Once she was all cried out, we decided to get organized and come up with a plan. Tara loved plans and lists. She thrived when she had both, so I knew that taking control of the situation was exactly what Tara needed to help her move on from her grief and start the rebuilding process.

"I called and spoke to the insurance company," Tara informed me. "They warned me that between the holiday, which slows everything down, and the fact that the bookstore is at the center of an open police investigation, it may be a while before we get the go-ahead to repair and rebuild, but they are sending someone out today to do a preliminary report and take photos."

"That's good. It is important to at least get the claim open."

Tara nodded. "I spoke to Danny after I spoke to you. Most of the damage to the building is to the cat lounge, although the contents in the bookstore are a mess thanks to the water the fire department dumped on the entire structure. Danny thinks we should secure the place with some well-placed plywood to prevent looting, so he is going to talk to Finn about doing it. I imagine that Finn is going to stay in control of the building until the investigation is complete, but I trust Danny to know what to do, so I'm leaving that up to him to work out."

Wow. Tara trusting Danny with her baby was huge in my mind. Maybe their hanging out again had progressed a lot farther than either had revealed to anyone else so far.

"The loss of income is going to be significant because the week before Christmas is one of our busiest times of the year," Tara continued. "Luckily, we do have insurance to cover that, so while I'll need to work out the specifics with the adjuster, we should have money to get us by until the store can reopen."

It was a lot more important for Tara to have uninterrupted income; she lived on her own and had to pay the mortgage and monthly maintenance fee on her condo, whereas I had Cody and lived rent free. I wanted to be sure her income was covered first, but I figured I'd talk to her about that at another time. Right now, this was keeping her busy, and I was content to let her orchestrate things as she saw fit.

"I called to speak to Alex this morning," she added. "He and Willow are both pretty shaken up. He would most likely be dead if you hadn't gotten him out of there in time. Of course, he realized that right off, but I don't think it completely hit him until he'd had a chance to think about it a bit."

"We all owe a huge debt of gratitude to Wiley," I said.

"Alex mentioned that as well," Tara said. "He wants to do something for Wiley and his mom. I'm not sure how she'll feel about that, but Alex does have a lot of money and can afford to help them out a bit, so maybe you could talk to her about that when you see her."

"I will," I said. "I'm not sure how receptive she'll be to help, but maybe if they need something specific right now, she might be open to the idea."

Tara leaned back and tilted her head toward the ceiling. The poor thing looked exhausted.

"I guess we should let everyone know that book club will be canceled until further notice." Tara sighed.

"I think everyone will pretty much assume that," I assured her. "I know it feels like there is a lot to take care of, but the reality is, the next few weeks are probably going to consist of a whole lot of waiting around for someone else to do something before the next person in line can do their thing."

Tara slowly exhaled. "I know. It is going to be hard not to have somewhere to go every day. But it is Christmas, and I remember wishing I had more time to enjoy the season when we were so busy last year."

"So let's enjoy it. You know I haven't even started my Christmas shopping." I looked around the cabin. "And I need to finish packing up here so Cassie can move in, and we have Mr. Parsons's party next week." I paused to appreciate the brightly lit tree. "There is so very much to see too." God, I was going to miss this place. "And of course there is also the Santa killer who needs tracking down. I know Finn is on it, and I have every confidence in his ability to catch the guy, but I still think I'm going to head over to talk to Wiley and Jingles. You can come with me if you want."

"I'm going to meet up with Danny in a little while. Like I said, he is going to help me figure out how to secure the building, so the things inside the bookstore that weren't destroyed aren't stolen before we are able to remove them. I'll also need to figure out where to temporarily store whatever we manage to salvage. I'm actually hoping Finn will let Danny and me clear out the storage room right away, but there was talk of structural integrity, so I guess we'll have to see how that goes." Tara leaned forward and hugged me. "Thanks for having me over this morning. I really needed to talk everything through. I felt so lost and helpless when I first woke up, but then I talked to you and then Danny, and then we met and worked out a plan of action, I feel better now."

I smiled. "I'm glad. And I'm glad Danny is helping with the inventory. To be honest, the fact that someone might get into the building through the damaged wall and steal whatever wasn't destroyed never even entered my mind."

"Mine either," Tara admitted. "At first. But then my mind went into overdrive, and I started to imagine every possible scenario. I even began to worry about someone breaking in to rob us getting hurt and then suing us because we didn't take precautions to stop people from breaking in and getting hurt."

As ridiculous as that sounded, I wasn't sure that Tara's concern was all that far off.

"I was going to head next door and check in with Cassie and Siobhan before I head into town," I informed Tara. "Do you want to come along?"

She nodded. "I do. I want to check on Cassie. I know she wasn't there when the bomb went off, but she has temporarily lost her only source of income. I want to assure her that we are going to take care of that."

"Cassie can probably pick up some shifts at the bar, and she has a place to live rent-free," I pointed out. "I think she'll be fine. But it might be nice if all of us talked things out. Willow too. She doesn't need to worry about the income, but I'm sure she is feeling as displaced as the rest of us. Maybe we should all meet to discuss things at some point."

Chapter 18

I drove over to Jane's after Tara left. I was anxious to check in with Wiley and Jingles. I hoped that Wiley would have a new drawing for me. Something that might make the drawing he gave me yesterday make sense.

"So, how did Jingles do last night?" I asked Jane when she answered the door and invited me in.

"Excellent. I tucked both Wiley and Jingles into Wiley's bed last night at around eight, and they both slept in until almost eight this morning. After the rough night Wiley had the night before, he really needed to have a good night's sleep, which he did. Which we both did."

"I'm so glad." I smiled.

"How are you doing after yesterday's events?" Jane asked.

"I will admit that now that things are beginning to sink in, I feel pretty out of sorts. But I also realize I don't have time to sit around feeling sorry for myself.

The most important thing is that no one was hurt, and I need to focus on that and not let the rest get me down. Besides, Jingles and I still need to help Finn track down the person behind these fires. From past experience, I know that the cats I work with have their own timeline, but I am hoping that Jingles will have a new clue for me today."

"Both Wiley and Jingles have been really quiet today. They came down for breakfast shortly after waking, but they've been back up in Wiley's room staring out the window quite contently ever since. I'm fine with you going up to check in with them."

"I'd like to do that."

I followed Jane up the stairs. As she'd said, the cat and the boy were sitting on the bed looking out the window. When I arrived, Jingles jumped down and crossed the room to greet me, but Wiley never looked in my direction.

"Good morning, Jingles," I said to the cat, who was doing circle eights between my legs.

"Meow."

I bent over and picked him up. "I don't suppose you have a new clue for me today?"

The cat put a paw on my cheek but didn't answer.

I glanced at Jane. "Have there been any new drawings?"

"Not since you were here yesterday."

I glanced at Wiley, who was still staring out the window. "Is he looking at something?"

"I don't know. I suspect that he is staring off into the distance while his mind is elsewhere, but I don't know what he is thinking about. I haven't noticed anything particularly interesting going on out the window this morning."

I glanced around the room. Someone, probably Jane, had picked up the drawings that had been strewn all around the room yesterday and stacked them neatly on a table.

"The tall man with the scribbled-out face that Wiley drew several times in the past couple of days: Has he drawn him before?"

Jane paused. "I don't know. He does draw a lot of really dark stuff sometimes. I find it disturbing, so most of the time I ignore it. I have a closetful of drawings we can look through if you are interested. I will admit that my first impression of the man without a face—that he was the person who set the fire at the Santa House—has changed somewhat."

"And why is that?" I asked.

"Initially, we talked about Wiley having seen someone but hadn't gotten a glimpse of his face because it was dark. That made sense in isolation. It is possible that the person who set fire to the Santa House passed by his window at some time. But the same figure was in the picture at the bookstore, and the man without a face was standing behind a woman with long hair in another picture as well. He couldn't actually have seen anyone in either of those situations. The man with the scribble-out face must exist in his mind."

I paused and watched Wiley for a moment. He hadn't moved, but he did look to be at peace. Wherever he was in his mind, he seemed to be happy there. "Do you think Wiley would mind if we looked at some of his drawings from the past few weeks?"

"I don't think he'll mind." Jane walked over to the closet, which contained hundreds of drawings. She took a pile from the top. "I just keep piling them in here, so these should be the more recent drawings. Well, except for the ones he's done in the past couple of days, which are all in the pile on the table."

I began to sort through the drawings. Some were dark and featured monsters, blood, and graveyards, but others were bright and colorful. There were drawings of puppies and rainbows as well as of disfigured creatures that moved around in the night. There were also drawings of random images: a hairbrush, a broom leaning against a wall, even a plate with two fried eggs sitting on it.

"Have you ever been able to decipher why he draws what he does? I mean, like the plate with the eggs. Was he just hungry when he drew that?"

"Sometimes I have a good idea why he chooses to draw the things he does, and other times, I have no idea. Like these." Jane pulled out a series of drawings of a puppy. "I'd taken Wiley for a walk in the park on the day he drew these. There was a woman there with a golden retriever puppy. Wiley didn't appear to be particularly interested in it. I didn't notice him watching or even looking at it. But when we got home, he drew at least twenty pictures of the puppy. Other times, I'm not sure where the ideas come from. Like this one." She held up a drawing of a red bike on a blue cloud floating over a green sea with a pink raft floating on top of it. "I have no idea where any of this came from. The thing that really stood out to me about this drawing was the colors. Most of Wiley's drawings are pencil drawings in black and white. When he does add color, it is usually subtle. But this is a rainbow of color."

Jane continued to sort through the drawings, stopping to point out a few along the way. When she came to a drawing of the people who'd drowned in the car, she paused. "The man with no face again," she said, handing me the drawing.

I took it from her and looked closely at the pencil drawing. The car, with four people inside, was covered with water, and the picture was very clearly drawn to the point where you could see the panic in their faces. In the background, there was an image hidden amid the grass growing beneath the waterline: a thin figure with no face.

I held up that drawing. "So either the same person was responsible for the fire at the Santa House and the death of these four people, which I highly doubt, or the tall man with the scribbled-out face represents something a bit more general. Maybe the image represents evil. Or maybe death. Maybe it is what he uses to represent fear or foreboding. I'm not sure we can know, but I do suspect that looking for a real man who is thin and tall and wears dark clothing would be a waste of time."

"I would tend to agree."

I set the drawing aside and looked at Wiley again. It didn't appear he'd moved an inch since I'd come into the room. "I was talking with some friends last night about everything that has been going on. We were trying to determine whether the fact that Wiley made drawings of Santa in the boat and the wall of locked drawers, both of which turned out to actually exist, indicates that whatever Tom Miller was doing with the boat and the items that were locked in the cabinets were connected to his death. Do you think he would have drawn them if the boat and the things in the drawers weren't related?"

Jane shrugged. "I have no idea. As I said, don't know why he draws what he does. I suppose whatever Mr. Miller was doing might be instrumental in determining why he was killed, but I believe it is equally possible that Wiley was simply focusing in on the man wearing the Santa suit, and he picked up those images in his mind."

Okay, I supposed that did provide a bit of clarity. If it was possible that Wiley had drawn Tom in his boat and the wall of locked cabinets in the boat just because they were connected to Tom, and Wiley had only been picking up images associated with Tom because he'd been focused on Santa and Tom just happened to have been acting as Santa, that meant we didn't have to limit ourselves to suspects known to Tom.

After chatting with Jane a bit longer, I decided to continue to leave Jingles with Wiley for the time being. She assured me that if either Jingles or Wiley became agitated or showed any signs of distress, she would call me. I planned to call her later to check in regardless.

I headed to Finn's office straight from Jane's house. I wasn't certain he would have had time to obtain any new information since last night, but I figured it couldn't hurt to ask.

"I do have something to tell you," Finn informed me after I'd sat down on the other side of his desk and asked for an update. "I took some time to go through the letters and journals I found on Tom's boat, and from what I have been able to gather, it appears that someone stole a load of silver bullion back in the 1950s," Finn began. "The journal that mentions it doesn't say where the silver was stolen from or who stole it, but it sounds as if the individual used the silver to make the counterfeit coins and then hid them. Perhaps the coins were earmarked for a specific use, or it could be the coins were a means of disguising the stolen silver. The journal doesn't go into detail about why the coins were produced but never circulated, so we may never know the answer to that specific question."

"So Tom found the letters and journals and decided to look for the coins, which he must have had reason to believe were hidden on the island?"

"It appears, based on what I can extrapolate from the diaries from the fifties and the letters, that is exactly what happened. Tom left his own journal of sorts in which he wrote about stumbling upon the old letters and journals and recognizing certain landmarks. He chronicles buying the boat so that he could go after the coins, which he believed were buried on a deserted island nearby. Based on the fact that we found coins in his pocket, and another twenty or so on his boat, I am going to assume that he found the stash he was looking for. Unfortunately, he didn't name a location, but I suppose that if he was able to find the coins from clues left in the journals, someone else could have as well."

"So are we thinking that Tom's death had something to do with these coins?" I asked.

Finn bobbed his head slowly before answering. "I'm not sure. The coins have some value. The friend I sent them to told me they aren't particularly good fakes, but of course, the silver could be melted down, and at today's prices, if there are as many coins as the journal indicates, they'd be worth a pretty penny once melted down. Still, if someone found out about Tom's treasure and wanted it for themselves, it seems they would have chosen a less public method of killing him. The idea that the coins are the motive for Tom's murder doesn't quite work in my mind."

"If Tom found a buried treasure and someone wanted to steal it, it would make a lot more sense if the person who wanted Tom dead shot him and dumped his body in the sea." I leaned back in my chair. "Okay, so we can explain why Tom had old quarters in his pocket and what the key opened. We also can explain why Wiley might have drawn Santa on a boat. But I still don't feel like we are any closer to finding the killer."

"I agree."

"So what are you going to do with the quarters and the journals and letters?"

"I'm turning everything over to the sheriff, who will be sure they end up in the right hands."

I guessed that was the right thing to do. If the quarters were most likely not related to Tom's death, Finn certainly wouldn't want to waste precious time on a treasure hunt. "What about the bullet casing in Tom's pocket?"

"It fits the sort of gun someone might use as a hunting rifle. Hunting is not allowed anywhere on the island, but there are folks who live here and take their guns with them to hunt elsewhere. There is nothing about the shell that gives us any information that would lead back to the gun from which it was fired. Without additional information, the shell is worthless as a clue."

"So it seems we are back to square one. Did you talk to Phil Colton about the key to Coffee Cat Books?"

"I did. He has keys and alarm codes from a lot of the merchants on the island, who prefer the convenience of having him drop off their deliveries at his convenience. He keeps the keys and codes in a locked cabinet in the ferry office and swears he has never had a problem in the almost ten years he has been making deliveries from the ferry, though he did admit that it was conceivable that someone else who worked for the ferry system might have both knowledge of the cabinet and a means of accessing it."

"I don't suppose there is any way to narrow that down."

"Unless someone saw something or knows something, not really."

"At this point, it seems that Wiley and Jingles have the best chance of leading us down the path we need to follow. I plan to check in with Jane later. When I was there this morning it was pretty quiet, so my gut tells me that if there is going to be a big reveal, we haven't yet reached the time for it. I'm going to go check in with Cody. I have my cell with me if something comes up or you need me for any reason."

"I'll call you. And let me know if either Wiley or Jingles come up with anything you feel is relevant."

I paused. "Maybe you should have Jane's cell number just in case something happens and I don't answer." I jotted down her number and passed it to Finn.

He picked it up. His eyes grew wide. "This is the cell number for Wiley's mother?"

"Yes. She has an out-of-state cell number."

Finn opened his desk drawer and pulled out a slip of paper with the same number, minus the area code. "This is the phone number we found in Tom's pocket."

Chapter 19

"No. I never met the man in my life," Jane assured us when Finn and I went to her house to ask her about the fact that it appeared that Tom had her cell number in his pocket "I have no idea why he would have my phone number, assuming it is my number. Keep in mind that without the area code, you can't know for certain."

"Maybe not," Finn admitted. "But the fact that Jingles led Cait to Tom's house, which caused her to call me to let her in, and together we found several items in the pocket of a pair of pants in Tom's laundry, I'm going to go out on a limb and say it was the phone number the cat wanted us to find. Especially because the other items in his pocket aren't panning out as having anything to do with his murder."

Jane just stood there, shaking her head.

"Maybe Tom was planning to approach Jane about something, but he never had the chance to do it," I suggested. "Maybe someone known to both Tom and Jane provided him with the number."

"What would the guy want with me?" Jane asked.

"Maybe he'd somehow heard about Wiley's unique talent. Perhaps after he drew the image of the people drowning in the car, and then they did," I suggested. "Did you tell anyone about the drawing?"

Jane nodded slowly. "Actually, I did. I was with my friend, Veronica, when the news came on, and I learned about the family that had drowned. I mentioned that Wiley had drawn that exact image during the overnight hours, which must have been shortly after the accident occurred. Normally, I protect Wiley from gawkers, so I keep his situation to myself, but Veronica is a close friend. She has supported me over the years when things have been tough, and I really needed a friend, so I guess I let my guard down and blurted out the first thing that popped into my head. After I'd revealed that fact, Veronica was, of course, interested in other things that Wiley had drawn that turned out to happen in real life. I shared a few instances with her. I guess I shouldn't have."

"Do you know if Veronica knew Tom Miller?" I asked.

"I have no idea. It never came up. But even if she did know him, why would she tell him about Wiley?"

"I don't know. Perhaps we should ask her."

Jane called Veronica, who admitted that she had spoken to Tom, who happened to be her next-door neighbor. She wasn't trying to betray Jane's trust, but Tom had lost his wife a while back and was having a hard time dealing with it. In a moment of despair, he'd shared his anguish with Veronica, and on a whim, she'd given him Jane's number. She admitted that she didn't understand what Wiley did or how he did it, but it appeared he had some sort of psychic ability, so she thought that maybe Wiley could help Tom connect with the woman his heart bled for. Jane explained that Wiley was not a medium and couldn't have helped Tom even if he'd lived. I could see that Jane was irritated with what Veronica had done, but it was clear she didn't want to damage their friendship by making a big deal out of what she had done, so she'd decided to let it go.

"Well, I guess that answers that question," I said.

Finn nodded and looked at Jane. "I'm sorry to have bothered you."

"No problem. I know how important it is to figure this out. And to be honest, I'm glad to have had a reminder to keep Wiley's talents to myself. The last thing I want is for him to become a spectacle."

"Cait and I and our friends will keep Wiley's talent to ourselves," Finn assured her.

I said goodbye to Jane once again, promising to check in at the end of the day. Learning what we had hadn't brought us any closer to Tom's killer, but perhaps it had led us a step closer to deciding that the killer had been after Santa and not necessarily after Tom.

Finn returned to his office, and I went next door to chat with Cody. His car was parked in front of the newspaper office, so I knew he'd be there.

"Okay. I'll see you on Sunday," Cody was just saying into the phone as I walked in.

"See who on Sunday?" I asked.

"That was Sammy's father. He is being sent home early. He will be flying into Seattle on Sunday and wondered if I could meet him there to hand Sammy off. He is continuing on to Florida later that evening."

I knew I should be thrilled that Cody and I were getting an early reprieve, but suddenly I found I felt sad.

"I'm happy that Sammy will be able to spend Christmas with his father, but I am a little sad I won't get to see him in the baby's first Christmas jammies I bought him."

"We can put them on him early and take a photo," Cody suggested.

"I guess. I will miss the little guy, but I suppose with the move and Mr. Parsons's party and the murder investigation, it is for the best. I'm sure Sammy's dad is thrilled that he will be with his son for his first Christmas."

"He is thrilled," Cody confirmed. "If you aren't tied up tonight, I thought we could bundle Sammy up and take him into town. We can start our Christmas shopping, and I'm sure he'll like the lights and the music."

"That would be fun. What time do you want to go?"

"I should be done here by four. I can stop and get him from day care, and we can meet back at the cabin."

I leaned forward and kissed Cody on the lips. "Okay. I'll see you there."

It looked like I had a few hours of free time this afternoon, so I decided to head back to the cabin to finish my packing. I knew I was stalling, and that wasn't fair to either Cody or Cassie. Both had been so patient in giving me the time I needed. I'd hoped that if I waited a bit, I'd feel more ready to make the final move, but deep down inside, I supposed I knew I'd never be ready.

When I returned to the estate, I let Max, who'd come home with me, into the cabin, and then headed toward the cat sanctuary. Siobhan, Cassie, and I all pitched in to make sure the cats were cared for, and the facility kept clean. Cassie had taken on the brunt of the work as of late, and I supposed that now that I was moving next door, it made sense to allow her to continue to take the lead, with Siobhan and me helping out when we could.

"Hey, everyone," I greeted the cats, who came to greet me after I'd let myself inside. The place had been pretty empty before I picked up the cats from the kill shelter in Seattle, but now we were close to capacity once again. Of course, when I picked up the cats, I'd assumed that as soon as they were acclimated, we'd try them out in the cat lounge. I guessed now that wasn't going to be an option for quite some time. I'd do what I could to get them adopted in a timely manner, but at least they were safe and comfortable with us while they waited.

I headed into the nursery, where we had two mama cats, one who had delivered two days before and another who was ready to deliver at any moment. Most of the time, the cats did fine doing it on their own, but I liked to keep an extra-close eye on things when I knew their time was near.

It looked like Cassie had already cleaned up and fed everyone. She really had turned out to be a responsible young woman. There was a time during her teenage years when I'd worried about her lack of drive and commitment, but I supposed most teens went through a similar phase.

After I made sure to check on all our current residents, I went back to my cabin. *Cassie's cabin.* Just the thought of it not being mine made me want to cry. I wasn't sure why I was having such a hard time with the move. I guess I wasn't the sort to embrace change. I paused when I entered the main floor of the cabin. Cody had packed up and moved everything I'd earmarked. All I still needed to do was grab Sammy's portable crib, formula, diaper bag, and a few other items we had left for the last minute, as well as a handful of clothes still left for me to take when I was ready. Two carloads and I'd be done.

I glanced at Max. "Are you ready?"

He wagged his tail.

I knew Max would enjoy living in the same house as his best buddy, Rambler. I also knew that now that Mr. Parsons was back from staying with Balthazar Pottage during the remodel, Cody was anxious to get back so the elderly man wouldn't be alone. I picked up a box Cody had left for me and started tossing clothes inside. Realizing this was never going to get any easier, I finally decided to just get it over with.

As predicted, it took me just two loads, and I was finally totally done. All that was left to do was to hand the keys over to Cassie and wish her happiness in her new home. I wasn't sure where she was today, so I called her cell.

"Hey, Cassie. I'm finally all moved and ready to give you the keys."

There was a pause. "Really? Are you sure?"

"I'm sure."

It was clear she was trying to rein in her happiness because she knew how hard this had been for me, but

I didn't miss the little screech of happiness over the phone line.

"I'm helping Danny and Tara board up the bookstore," she informed me. "We were going to head over to the bar after. I can come home if you want."

"No. That's okay. I'll come to you. I'll be there in twenty minutes."

I called Cody to let him know what I was doing. He seemed surprised as well. I told him I'd just bring the stroller and warm clothes for Sammy if he wanted to pick him up and meet me at the bar. We'd change Sammy and go into town from there.

Chapter 20

When I arrived at the bookstore, the destruction hit me like a ton of bricks. I hadn't stopped to take a second look after leaving the previous day. In fact, when I'd come into town, I'd taken an alternate route to avoid the bookstore completely.

"Wow," I said as I stood in front of the building.

Cassie hugged me tightly. "That was exactly what I said when I arrived earlier. Are you okay?"

I nodded.

"If you need to wait a few days on the cabin, I'm fine with that."

I smiled. "No. I'm ready." I reached into my pocket, pulled out the keys, and handed them to her. "May you be as happy in the cabin as I've been."

Cassie couldn't help but grin. She hugged me again. "I'm sure I will be."

I looked back toward the bookstore. It felt easier than dwelling on the whole moving thing. "It looks like you guys have made a lot of progress."

"Tara is a woman on a mission. Danny and I just did what she told us to do, and everything came together rather quickly. We are almost done, and then we are leaving for the bar. Do you want to come?"

"I do. Cody and I are taking Sammy into town to see the lights later, but he is going to meet me at the bar."

"I think after today, we'll all enjoy a drink," Cassie said.

At the bar, Danny went to work and Tara, Cassie, and I found a booth in the back. Shortly after we arrived, Willow showed up. It was good that the four of us had a chance to sit and process everything together.

"I still can't believe what happened really happened," Tara said. "It feels like a bad dream."

"I know what you mean," Willow said. "I had nightmares all night. I'm just so grateful that everyone got out safely. Alex was sitting right next to the package, and I wasn't all that far away from it. I can't bear to think about what could have happened."

"It was a miracle that Cait happened to see the drawing and connected the dots in time," Cassie agreed.

"We all owe our lives to Wiley," I said. "If he hadn't given me that drawing, I would never have realized there was a problem."

"Any news on the Tom Miller front?" Willow asked.

I took a few minutes to catch everyone up. I shared what Finn had told me, my conversations with Jane, and the fact that it looked as if someone with a grudge against Santa and not one against Tom might actually have carried out the attack on the Santa

House, as we'd been thinking. We all shared our concerns for any additional Christmas events that might still be scheduled on the island. I shared with Willow, who hadn't been at last night's meeting, Siobhan's intention to try to get everyone who planned to have a Santa to change their plans.

"Any idea when we will be back up and running?" Willow asked once we'd exhausted the subject of Santas and suspects.

"I have no idea," Tara answered. "I don't think anything is going to be done about our insurance claim until after the first of the year. Someone did come by to take photos, but even they mentioned that they were off after tomorrow for two full weeks. As badly as I want to dig in and start doing everything we need to do to get the store open again, I think it is going to be a while."

"I guess that will give me more time with Alex and Barrington," Willow said, referring to her son, who'd been named after his biological father. "Maybe Barry and Sammy can have a play date."

"Actually, Sammy is going home on Sunday," I informed the others. I explained that his father was being sent home and that Cody was meeting him at the airport to hand the baby off.

"You must be relieved," Cassie said.

"You know, after all the complaining I've done, you would think that would be true, but I think I'm actually going to miss the little guy. Having a baby to take care of is hard work, but there is something rewarding about it as well. I'd already bought him some Christmas gifts. I'm happy he will be with his daddy for Christmas, but I am feeling a little sad as well."

"You could always have your own little bundle of joy," Cassie said.

"I'm not feeling that sad." I smiled at Cassie. "Besides, I'm going to be too busy for a baby. I have a new home to settle in to, and as soon as we are able, Tara is going to get the bookstore up and running."

"I am," Tara confirmed.

"Alex and I want to help," Willow said. "In any way we can. You are like family, and Coffee Cat Books is the whole reason we met. We want to be part of whatever needs to be done to get things back to normal."

"The four of us should continue to meet," Cassie suggested. "Maybe once a week for lunch. Just so we can all be in the loop about what is going on."

"I love that idea," Tara said.

"Me too," Willow said. "I'm going to miss seeing everyone at work."

"We'll still see one another all the time even if the store isn't open for a while," I said, directing my comment more toward Willow than the others because Cassie was my sister and Tara was my best friend, and we saw one another all the time outside of work. "We have Mr. Parsons's party coming up next week, and it seems like we all end up here at the bar pretty often."

"I'm looking forward to the party," Willow said. "I know Balthazar is as well. He really enjoyed having Mr. Parsons stay with him during the remodel. Alex and I visit him all the time, but I think he gets lonely with only Ebenezer to keep him company," she added, referring to his cat.

The four of us continued to chat and support one another in our time of grief. It was nice to feel that others shared your shock and pain. While Tara and I owned Coffee Cat Books, Cassie and Willow were connected to the store and had a commitment to the Coffee Cat Books family.

Eventually, Cody showed up with Sammy, and Willow left to get home to Alex and Barrington. Cassie wanted to start settling into her new home, and Tara planned to stay at the bar to hang out with Aiden and Danny. I felt bad for Tara. I knew the hole created by the loss of Coffee Cat Books was going to affect her most of all. I had a new home to settle in to, as did Cassie, and Willow had Alex, while I had Cody. But Tara seemed stagnant in her personal life and unsettled in more ways than one. I wasn't sure that a relationship with Danny was right for either one of them, but I did hope that he continued to be there for her during the next few difficult weeks.

Chapter 21

Sunday, December 22

Cody and Sammy had left on the first ferry to Anacortes. I might have gone with them, but today was the Christmas play at the church, and although Sister Mary had taken over as lead from Cody and me after the explosion at the bookstore, I still wanted to be there to support the kids. Some years Saint Patrick's put on a huge production that was held in the evening, but Cody and I knew our time would be limited this year because we had Sammy, so we'd decided from the beginning on a smaller production performed during Sunday Mass. The way things had turned out, I was extra glad we'd come to that decision ahead of time.

"Okay, everyone, remember to relax and have fun," I said to the kids as we got them ready to take the walk from the choir room to the church. Tara was also in attendance to help out, so while I missed Cody being there, we really didn't need him.

"Where is your baby?" Anastasia asked. "I thought you were going to bring him here for us to meet."

"Cody took Sammy to meet his daddy, who is arriving home early."

"So he isn't coming?"

"I'm afraid not."

"What about your cat?" Archie asked. "The one you were sleeping with at that rehearsal last week. Is he coming?"

"No. I'm sorry, he won't be here either. But both your parents are here. I noticed them earlier." I turned to Anastasia. "And your grandmother is here. In fact, when I peeked into the church earlier, it looked like we had a full house, so let's get lined up and ready to make our grand entrance."

"Is your mom here?" Anastasia asked.

"She is. And my brothers and sisters are here too. Ready, everyone?"

They all nodded that they were.

Thankfully, the play went off without a hitch. The kids remembered their lines for the most part, and with the exception of a baby angel who decided to add hip-hop moves to her song, everything went exactly as rehearsed. After church, Finn and Siobhan, Aiden and Danny, Cassie and Tara and I all went to the house my mom shared with her husband, Gabe, for Sunday lunch. We were halfway through the meal when Jane called to let me know that Wiley and Jingles had suddenly become upset. After several days of calm moods and smooth sailing, she was worried that another explosion might be on the horizon.

"I need to go," I said to my family. I then explained about the call.

"I'll come with you," Tara offered.

"I should go as well," Finn said.

"No. If everyone shows up, it might freak Wiley out. I'll go. I'll see if I can figure out what he is trying to say and then I'll call you to let you know."

"I'll drive you," Finn insisted. "I'll wait in the car if you think that is best, but I'm not leaving you to deal with whatever might be happening on your own."

"Okay," I agreed. "We'll call the rest of you when we know more."

I slid into the passenger seat of Finn and Siobhan's car. He was off duty today, so he didn't have his cruiser. I supposed that if we needed the others to take some sort of action, Siobhan could get a ride with Tara or Cassie.

"Have you spent any time with Wiley and Jingles since Thursday?" Finn asked.

"I've checked in with Jane every day and looked in on Jingles just to make sure that he didn't have something he needed to communicate to me, but both the boy and the cat have been quiet and content the past few days. When I poke my head in the door of Wiley's bedroom, he pretty much ignores me, and while Jingles trots over to say hi, he has been calm as well. Jane told me that Wiley and Jingles had a good night last night and that they seemed calm this morning, but then, about an hour ago, Wiley started drawing frantically and Jingles is crying and pacing."

Finn pulled up in front of Jane's home. I opened the passenger door. "I'll wait here so as not to upset Wiley further," he said, "but if you need me to come in, let me know."

"I will. I shouldn't be long. If Wiley is upstairs, it will probably be fine for you to come in and wait downstairs. I'll let you know what the situation is once I speak to Jane."

Jane answered as soon as I knocked on the door. Jingles ran out onto the front stoop, almost knocking me off my feet. Wiley was standing just inside the door. He was looking at the floor, but he was obviously waiting for me. He held out a drawing. I took it. The picture was of Santa in a chair with a gift with fire coming out of it next to him. I was pretty sure that everyone on the island who planned to have a Santa had canceled theirs, so I wasn't certain what Wiley was so worked up about.

I smiled at Wiley even though he wasn't looking at me. "Thank you, Wiley. I can see that there is another Santa in trouble. I'm afraid I don't know where this one is. Can you show me?"

Wiley turned away from me.

I looked down at Jingles. "I guess it's up to you. Do you know where we are heading?"

"Meow."

"Okay." I bent down and picked up the cat. "Let's go." I looked at Jane. "I'll call you when we figure this out. If Wiley shows you anything else that you think might help us, call me."

"I will. And good luck."

I slid back into the car with Jingles in my arms. I handed the paper to Finn. "Any idea where this might be?"

"No. As far as I know, all the local events that had been scheduled to include a Santa have canceled him."

"Okay, Jingles. It's up to you to lead the way."

Finn just stared at me. "How exactly is he going to lead the way?"

"Just start driving. We'll tell you when to turn."

When Jingles took us north, not toward town, both Finn and I were confused. The only buildings north of Harthaven were single-family homes. Most of the ones on the north shore were large estates, although there were a few smaller houses that had been on the island for generations.

Eventually, Jingles led us to a huge estate that was owned by a tech billionaire who worked out of Seattle. There were dozens of cars in the driveway.

"Private event," I said.

"Looks like it."

Finn parked, and he, Jingles, and I headed toward the front door. There were a lot of people inside, and the door was open, so we simply walked in. The main living area was packed with mingling adults in nice clothing. I didn't see a Santa, but Jingles ran down a hallway that led to a conservatory where a man dressed in a Santa suit was listening to children's wishes and then handing them each a gift.

"I need everyone to clear out," Finn demanded in his deep baritone voice.

"What's going on?" a man I assumed might be the homeowner demanded.

"I'm Ryan Finnegan, the resident deputy. A bomb threat has been called in. We have had two other bombings on the island recently involving Santas, so we have reason to believe it is authentic. Now, everyone out."

I ran into the conservatory and began shepherding the children out. Santa hesitated but finally followed them. Finn made a call, I assumed to the fire department, or perhaps for backup. Once everyone was out on the lawn, he turned to the owner. "Is there anyone else inside? Help? Guests? Anyone upstairs?"

"I don't know. There were a lot of people here."

I was holding Jingles, and now he squirmed out of my arms and headed back toward the house. "Jingles," I screamed.

He headed in through the open front door. I ran after him. I could hear Finn calling after me, but I needed to get the cat, but I knew that if he ran back in, someone was still inside. The cat took off up the stairs. I followed. I had just arrived on the second-floor landing when a loud explosion rocked the house. I fell to the floor but was far enough away from the blast that I was unharmed. Still, the house was on fire. I needed to get out of there.

"Jingles! Where are you?"

"Meow."

I ran toward the sound of the cat. At the end of the hallway was a bedroom. On the dresser was a photo of a blond-haired child sitting on Santa's lap with a blond woman standing beside them. It looked exactly like the drawing Wiley had made, minus the faceless man. I grabbed the photo and the cat and headed back down the stairs. Finn met me halfway up.

"Are you crazy?" he demanded.

"Apparently. Let's get out of here. I have what the cat wanted me to find."

The fire department showed up shortly after. While Finn coordinated with the emergency personnel, I sought out the owner of the home. I found him rounding everyone up and shepherding them toward the pool house to wait for further instructions.

"Can I speak to you for a moment?" I asked the man I now recognized as billionaire Theodore Stinson.

The poor guy looked harassed beyond belief, but he agreed. I showed him the photo. "What can you tell me about this photo?"

"The Santa is me. I hired someone to give out the gifts this year because my arthritis has been acting up, but until this year, I have always personally handed out the gifts to the children of my employees."

"And the woman?"

"Her name was Estelle Winters. She worked for me as my personal assistant when I first started my company. The child on my lap is her son, Devon. He currently works for me as a programmer."

"You said the name of the woman *was* Estelle Winters. I assume she passed away."

Stinson bowed his head. "She died shortly after this photo was taken. In fact, she passed out while I was still holding Devon. She was rushed to the hospital, but she'd had a heart attack and didn't make it. There was nothing they could do." The man frowned. "Where did you get this photo?"

"It was on the dresser in the upstairs bedroom at the back of the hallway."

"Devon is staying in that room. I guess he must have brought it with him." His forehead furrowed. "It seems odd that he kept this photo as a reminder of that day. Devon was only six when his mom died. His grandmother raised him for a while, but she became ill, and he went into the foster care system. When I found out about it, I paid for him to attend a private boarding school and then college. After he graduated, I hired him and made sure he was on the management path. Most Christmases, he stays with me for a few days when I bring the employees from my Seattle office to the island for a holiday party." He looked around. "I haven't seen him since the blast. I hope he got out all right."

"I'll help you look for him," I offered. "What does he look like?"

"Blond. Tall. He had on brown slacks and a green sweater."

"Thick hair, prominent cheekbones?"

"Yes. Did you see him?"

"I did earlier."

I had also seen him at the bookstore on the day of the explosion there, I realized. I couldn't be sure at this point, but given what I'd just found out, I suspected that Devon was the Santa killer. I couldn't explain why he might have gone over the edge and started killing Santas after all these years, but I could see how having your mother die right in front of you while you were sitting on Santa's lap could lead to a serious hatred of the jolly old elf in the red and white suit.

Chapter 22

As soon as the fire had been dealt with, I shared my theory with Finn, who shared it with a very reluctant Theodore Stinson. He didn't want to believe that Devon was behind the bombs, and I didn't blame him, but after Stinson showed me a photo of the man, I was able to confirm that he was indeed the one I'd seen lurking around on the day Coffee Cat Books exploded. Stinson also confirmed that Devon had arrived on the island early this month, and while Stinson had only just arrived himself the previous Friday, Devon had been staying at this house for the past two weeks. Finn asked if there had been others staying here as well, and Stinson replied that as far as he knew, it had only been Devon and the help on the estate until he got here on Friday.

"Any idea where he might be now?" Finn asked the man who insisted we call him Theo.

He slowly shook his head.

Despite a thorough search, Devon Winters had not been found, but Theo confirmed that one of his smaller boats was missing. We assumed that Theo had escaped during the confusion following the explosion.

"Do you have any idea why Devon might have done this?" Finn asked.

Theo started to shake his head, but then he stopped. "I guess you know that Devon's mother died of a heart attack right in front of him while he was visiting Santa?"

"Yes, Cait explained that to me," Finn confirmed.

"And she also told you that I was the one playing Santa when Estelle died?"

"Yes, she told me that as well," Finn confirmed. "And I can understand how that might affect a person, especially one so young. But that happened a long time ago. Do you have any idea what might have caused Devon to suffer a psychological break all these years later?"

Theo didn't answer right away. Then he said, "Devon was alone in the house for almost two weeks before I arrived. I suppose he might have decided to look around. I can't be sure until I'm able to get inside to take a look, but I suspect that he might have found the paperwork regarding the agreement his mother and I worked out when he was born. You see, Estelle was not only my personal assistant, she was my mistress, and Devon is my son. I was married at the time and still trying to grow my company. I was afraid a scandal would derail everything I'd worked so hard for, so I paid Estelle off in exchange for her promise never to reveal the identity of Devon's father." Theo ran his hand through his hair. "I've regretted my actions many times since then, but despite the fact that I considered telling Devon the truth on many occasions, I never have." He closed his eyes and groaned. "And the truth is even worse when you consider the pain I caused Estelle. The doctors felt her heart attack was most likely the result of drug abuse. She never took drugs until after Devon was born, and I denied his parentage. Her death really was my fault. I knew it then, and I know it now."

"So why did Estelle continue to work for you if you'd paid her off?" I asked.

"We wanted to keep up appearances, I wanted to stay close to Devon even though I refused to claim him as my own, and I believe that despite it all, Estelle never stopped loving me. I think she decided that being my assistant was better than not having a relationship with me at all. She no longer needed the money, but she continued to work alongside me until the day she died." Theo looked at Finn. "We need to find Devon. In his present state of mind, there is no telling what he might do."

I could see that Finn was going to be busy for a while with the cleanup and witness interviews, so I called Tara to ask if she could pick up Jingles and me. She arrived in her SUV, along with Siobhan and Cassie. Mom had volunteered to babysit Connor, and Danny and Aiden planned to meet us at the bar where we could talk in private because O'Malley's was closed on Sundays. When we arrived back in Harthaven, I asked Tara to stop at Jane's so I could leave Jingles there.

"So, you arrived in time?" she asked.

"We did," I confirmed. "No one was hurt, and I'm pretty sure we identified the man behind the fires, thanks to Wiley and his drawings."

"I'm glad it worked out okay. Is the man in jail?"

"Not yet, but Finn will find him." I looked down at the cat in my arms. "I suspect that Jingles's job may be done, so I am going to leave him with you. If it turns out I do need him, I'll call, but I think you can consider him a permanent part of your family now."

Jane thanked me, and I passed the cat to her. Wiley walked up behind his mother, and the cat struggled to get down. She set him on the floor, and both the cat and the boy ran up the stairs.

"Did you ever figure out who the man with the scribbled-out face was?" Jane asked.

"I don't think the man represents a person. I think it is the image of death. In all the drawings of a man with no face, someone has either died or would have died if Wiley and Jingles hadn't warned us of the impending death." I reached out and touched Jane on the arm. "I'm sure knowing what Wiley does is a heavy burden to bear, and it is difficult for you as his mother as well. I just want you to know I am always here for you both. If Wiley starts having nightmares or if he begins to draw things that come true, you can call me anytime, day or night. In fact, call me anyway. I'd like us to be friends."

Jane smiled. "I'd like that too."

I reached over and hugged her. "Alex wants to do something for you and Wiley. He wanted me to ask you if there was anything you needed."

Jane hesitated.

"Wiley saved Alex's life. He wants to thank him. And he has a lot of money, so if there is anything at all…"

"Wiley does need a new computer. The one he has is on its last legs."

"That's perfect. I'll let Alex know, and we'll bring it by when we have it."

"That would be nice. The past few weeks have been hard, but it has been nice having you and the others pop in from time to time. Being Wiley's mother is very rewarding, but it can be lonely at times."

"Honestly, I'd be happy to continue popping in. I like to keep track of the cats I hand off to others, and I've enjoyed getting to know you. Maybe we can make a weekly thing of it."

"I'd like that very much."

I turned to walk away. "I'm not sure how Wiley would do with a roomful of people, but we are having a big Christmas Eve party if you and Wiley are interested in coming."

Jane hesitated. "I suppose I could broach the subject with him. Can I call you and let you know?"

"Absolutely. I'll text you the details." If I hadn't had a carful of people waiting for me, I might have stayed longer, but I did, so I said my goodbyes and promised to text her later in the day.

"So is that it?" Tara asked after I returned to the car, and we headed toward the bar to meet Danny and Aiden for a drink. "Are the Santas of Madrona Island safe now?"

"I hope so. The logic Finn and I used to decide that Devon was the man we were looking for seems solid, but until Finn tracks him down and gets him to confess, we can't know for sure. Still, I did see him at the bookstore when the cat lounge was blown up, and he did leave during the confusion today, so I would say that assuming he is the man we've been looking for is a safe bet."

"I have to admit that I feel bad for him," Cassie said. "Not that I am saying he was in any way justified for doing what he's done, but it must have been tough to lose his mother at such a young age and then find out all those years later that the man he most likely looked up to was the father who'd turned his back on him when he'd needed him the most."

"Yeah. My heart does hurt for the guy. I just hope they can track him down and get him the help he needs."

Chapter 23

Tuesday, December 24

"Oh my gosh, I'm so happy you came." I hugged Jane when she arrived at Mr. Parsons's Christmas Eve party with Wiley in tow. Jingles, who was surprisingly walking politely on a leash held by Wiley, had come along as well.

"Wiley seemed to be okay with it when I explained what we were going to do. We can always leave if it doesn't work out. I hope it is okay that we brought Jingles. He seems to have a calming effect on Wiley. We've started taking him with us when we go on our walks, and I find that with Jingles along, Wiley is able to deal with people, noise, and confusion a lot better."

"Of course it is okay that you brought Jingles." I motioned for Cassie to join us. "This is my sister, Cassie. She'll show you where to hang your coats, where to find beverages, and where to sit if you want to find somewhere quiet. My older sister, Siobhan, is in the parlor with some of the kids if you want to try that. Dinner will be served in a half hour or so."

Jane greeted Cassie, who led her down the hallway. I was so happy to see that both Jane and Wiley had decided to show up. I hoped it went well. If Jingles could help Wiley deal with social situations, that would really open up the world for Jane, who seemed to have been living a fairly solitary life when I met her.

"Francine wants to know when you want her to start setting out the food on the buffet tables," Danny asked me.

"In about thirty minutes. Services should be over at Saint Patrick's by now, but I want to give Sister Mary and the others time to get here. Is Aiden still manning the bar?"

"He is. You know he is in his element behind the bar."

"I know, and it was nice of the two of you to donate the alcohol so we could offer an open bar in addition to the wine."

"I think everyone is having a really good time, and Aiden is monitoring the amount of alcohol he serves so no one has too much. In fact, the Christmas punch that has been so popular is mostly punch."

"That's probably a good thing. Have you seen Cody?"

"He is helping in the kitchen. I should get back there, as well. I know that Francine, Siobhan, Mom, and Maggie have things handled, but there is a lot of lifting and carrying to take care of, which is where Cody and I come in."

Mr. Parsons's Christmas Eve party started off as a way for Cody and me to spend part of our holiday with our elderly neighbor despite our family obligations. That first year, we'd planned a small dinner party that had grown to over sixty people after we began inviting others who might not have had a place to go. This year, we'd be serving dinner for over a hundred. While Mr. Parsons was a bit of a recluse, he seemed to really enjoy the annual event, and Cody and I were happy to make it happen.

"Did I see Jane and Wiley come in?" Alex asked.

I smiled at the adorable toddler in his arms. "They are here. Cassie took them to grab something to drink, and then I think she was going to take them to Siobhan, who is with the kids in the parlor."

"Great. I wanted to see how the computer I got for Wiley was working out. When I delivered it to him, I swear I saw him smile."

"He doesn't smile often, but I've seen him smile at Jingles, so he might have. Does he know how to use it?"

"And how. The kid is a savant. I think having a newer and more powerful window on the world is going to help him a lot." Alex looked down at Barrington. "Should we go find Connor?"

Barrington smiled an adorable two-toothed grin. It seemed that he felt that was a very good idea indeed.

"By the way, did Finn track down Devon?" Alex asked.

I nodded. "He was picked up at the airport in Seattle. Finn hasn't spoken to him personally, but he did indicate that he was cooperating. I guess, as we suspected, he went a little bit crazy when he realized that the man he knew as a father figure was really the father who had not only failed to claim him but had most likely been responsible for his mother's anguish, eventually leading to her death."

Alex slowly shook his head. "The whole thing is just so sad."

"I couldn't agree more."

Alex and Barrington went off to find Jane and Wiley, and I headed toward the kitchen to check on the crew there. Everyone was pitching in, and it looked as if they had everything prepared and transferred to serving dishes.

"I noticed Sister Mary drive up, so go ahead and start setting the food out on the buffet tables. I'll let everyone know they can come in to dinner."

Once the hundred-plus guests were seated at the long tables we'd set up in the ballroom, Maggie's husband, Michael, who'd been a priest before he was a husband, said grace. I felt a warmth in my heart as family and friends from six months to over eighty years in age gathered together to break bread while taking a moment to celebrate the birth of a very special baby. Some of the people in the room were Christian, and some were not, but whatever their religious beliefs, I knew that everyone who'd gathered believed in the friendship and caring that spanned the generations. While Christmas may be about gift-giving for many people, I knew deep in my heart that love and the expression of that love through our acts of kindness was the greatest gift of all.

Up Next from Kathi Daley Books

https://amzn.to/2luDyDL

Preview

Friday, November 16

You know what they say about the best-laid plans?

I was on my way to a weekend getaway with Trevor Johnson, one of my two best friends, when I got a call from Officer Woody Baker. Woody was a good guy who'd helped me out on more than one occasion, so when he asked for my help in tracking down the man who'd shot a local social worker, I didn't feel I could turn him down in spite of the fact that Trevor and I were still trying to recover from the worst cruise in history. Well, maybe not the worst in history; I did remember the Titanic. But while our cruise may not have been quite as bad as that history-making cruise gone wrong, it definitely wasn't the relaxing time I'd been promised by my other best friend, Mackenzie Reynolds, and her new guy friend, Ty Matthews. Not only had I run into a ghost on my second night aboard, but the ship had been hijacked, and other passengers had ended up dead before the nightmare at sea was over as well.

"My name is Amanda Parker. Officer Baker sent me," I said to the woman at the front desk of the hospital. "I'm here to meet Carmen Rosewood."

The woman looked down at her log. "Yes. Ms. Rosewood is waiting for you. Just take the elevator to the second floor and then make a left. Trinity Rosewood is in room 202."

Offering the woman a look of thanks, I headed toward the elevator. I really doubted, due to the unique circumstance, that I'd be able to help Woody accomplish what he hoped, but I knew I needed to try.

"Carmen Rosewood?" I asked the dark-haired woman sitting next to the hospital bed currently occupied by Trinity Rosewood.

"Yes." The woman nodded. "You must be Amanda Parker."

"I am. I'm sorry about your sister."

A tear rolled down the woman's face. "Who would do this to Trinity? She's a good person who spent her life helping others. This whole thing makes no sense."

I offered the woman a gentle smile. "I know. I'm sorry." I glanced at the woman currently hooked up to a variety of monitors and machines. "Has there been any change?"

Carmen slowly shook her head. "According to the doctor, all we can do is wait. Either Trinity will fight to live or she won't. There really isn't anything more the doctors can do at this point."

"I've never had the pleasure of meeting Trinity, but Woody assures me she is a fighter."

Carmen offered me a tiny smile. "She is. If anyone can survive this, it will be Trinity." She glanced away from her sister and toward me. "I'm not sure why Officer Baker wanted you to spend time with Trinity, but he asked me to allow you to sit with her for a while, and I agreed." She stood up. "If you are some sort of a psychic or healer, please do everything you can. I'll be in the waiting room. You can just come and get me when you are finished."

"Thank you. I won't be long."

Sitting in the chair Carmen had just vacated, I realized all I could do at this point was to open my mind and wait. Woody is a fantastic cop who doesn't normally need help to do his job, but the shooting in question took place after dark in the driveway of the woman's home, and no one had seen who'd pulled the trigger except for the woman herself. The problem was that Trinity was in a coma and couldn't tell anyone what had happened. Given the fact that I could see and speak to ghosts, Woody hoped I might be able to communicate with her. I agreed to try, but ghosts were dead, and this woman was simply unconscious, so I really doubted it would work.

"Trinity. Are you here?" I asked in a gentle voice. "Can you hear me?"

There was no response. I looked at the monitors which seemed to be beeping along steadily. Trinity looked to be at peace. She didn't appear to be close to death. I honestly doubted that I would be able to connect with her. Deciding to see if my alter ego Alyson was around, I silently called out to her. She appeared.

"Can you sense her?" I asked in a quiet voice.

"No," the half of me that existed in spirit form replied. "The woman is still very much alive. Her essence has not separated from her body. I guess that is a good thing, but I'm not sure there is a lot you and I can do at this point."

I nodded. "I thought as much, but I had to try. I'm going to wait here for a few minutes just in case we're wrong and Trinity is trying to reach out to us."

Alyson disappeared, and I reached out and took the woman's hand in my own. "My name is Amanda. I'm not sure if you can hear me, but if you can, I'm here to help you. I can't stay long, but I will be back tomorrow. If you can find a way to communicate with me, I want you to know that you don't have to be afraid of me. I only want to help."

Trinity didn't move, but I sensed that my message had been received. I stood and walked out into the waiting room.

"So?" Carmen asked.

"Your sister is at peace. She is strong. I didn't sense distress. I wasn't able to speak with her directly today, so I'd like to come back tomorrow. Honestly, I'm not sure I can do anything to help Trinity, but I'd like to try."

"Yes. Of course. Please feel free to come back any time. Officer Baker didn't go into any detail, but he did say that you have a unique gift and might be able to help."

"I'll do what I can."

Once I returned to my car, I called Woody from my cell.

"Well?" he asked.

"Trinity is very much alive and is not even close to separating from her spirit. I do plan to return tomorrow and try again, but at this point, I think we are going to need another way to identify the person who shot her."

I could hear Woody breathing, but he didn't answer right away. Eventually, he spoke. "Yeah. I've been working on it, but I'm not really getting anywhere. I don't suppose you'd like to grab some lunch and we could talk it through. At this point, I feel like I've hit a dead end."

"I'd be happy to talk it through with you. I'll grab some sandwiches and meet you at your office. We can eat and chat in the conference room where we won't be interrupted or overheard."

"Great. And thank you."

"Anytime."

Once I hung up with Woody, I called Trevor.

"Any luck?" he asked.

"No, but given the fact that I can see and speak to ghosts, that is a good thing. Alyson seemed to feel that at this point, the woman is well connected to her spirit. I'm going to head over and chat with Woody about the case. Do you want to come?"

"Yeah. I'd like that. Do you want to meet at Woody's office?"

"That would be great. I'm going to pick up some sandwiches. I should be there in twenty minutes or so."

After I hung up with Trevor, I headed toward the deli. After our cruise from hell ended early, Trevor and I had decided to spend a few days touring the San Juan Islands while Mac and Ty went off on their own romantic holiday. Trevor and I had been skirting the *friends* versus *something more than friends* issue for a while now, and I was sorry we hadn't had the chance to really explore our options. Not that I would have considered turning Woody down when he'd asked for my help, but it did seem that Trevor and I were destined to remain in the friend zone for all eternity. And maybe that was a good thing. Maybe taking our relationship to the next level would end in disaster. Trevor had been one of my best friends, along with Mac, since I'd first moved to Cutter's Cove as a teenager in witness protection. He meant a lot to me. More than I'd even realized until I'd returned to Cutter's Cove ten years after having left when witness protection ended. Was I really willing to risk that friendship by exploring a romance? I knew deep in my heart that once you crossed the line between friendship and romance, you could never really go back.

"Two Italian subs and a veggie sub," I said to the man behind the counter at the deli.

"Coming right up."

Walking over to the cooler, I grabbed three sodas. The place was pretty deserted today, but I supposed it was because it was a weekday during the off-season when the town as a whole tended to be somewhat deserted.

"Chips?" the man asked.

"No. Just the sandwiches and these sodas." I picked up the regional newspaper and an image of a man being shot flashed into my mind. Okay, that was odd. My superpower seemed to be to see and speak to ghosts so I could help them do whatever it was they needed to do to move on. I didn't have premonitions. At least I hadn't until now if that is even what was going on. Of course, I'd had prophetic dreams in the past. I supposed that flashes of insight were really nothing more than an extension of that. "I'll take this newspaper as well," I added.

Once I paid the man, I headed toward Woody's office. Trevor's truck was already there.

"I hope Italian subs are okay," I offered a sandwich and soda to each man.

"Sounds perfect to me," Woody replied. "Are Mac and Ty coming as well?"

"They are currently sequestered away at an undisclosed location getting their romance on," Trevor said.

"We can call or text if we need them, but let's only bother them if we really need their help," I suggested.

"Sounds fine to me," Woody said as he opened his soda. "I really want to thank the two of you for dropping everything to help out."

"We're always happy to do what we can." I opened the paper and turned to page two. I laid the paper on the table and pointed to a photo of a tall man dressed in a dark suit. "What can you tell me about this man?"

Woody looked at the photo. "His name is Bryson Teller. He is an attorney specializing in family law and child custody. Why do you ask?"

"While I was at the deli, I picked up the newspaper and had a flash of this man being shot."

Woody raised a brow. "Do you think it was a premonition?"

"I honestly don't know. I have had prophetic dreams in the past, but nothing like this. Whatever happened, if anything actually happened, is brand new. Still, given everything else, I do think we might want to take my flash seriously."

"I'll call him," Woody offered.

Trevor and I waited while Woody looked up and then dialed the law office where the man worked. He was told that Bryson was in court, so he left a message.

"I'm not sure what more I can do at this point," he said after hanging up.

"Where did the shooting take place?" Trevor asked.

Furrowing my brow, I answered. "I'm not sure. The whole thing really caught me off guard, and I didn't really pay much attention to the details. If it happens again, I'll be ready, and I'll try to notice the details." I opened my soda. "Would Trinity and Bryson have worked together on the same cases?"

"Sure," Woody said. "As a social worker, Trinity's job is to do whatever is in the best interest of the individuals in her care. Sometimes that means prosecuting others who wish to do harm to those she has been entrusted to protect, whether it be children, the elderly, or those who are unable to act as an advocate for themselves."

"I think we should take this flash seriously, especially given what happened to Trinity," I said. "I know the man is in court, but there must be a way to get a message to him."

"I can try," Woody said. "I'm just not sure what to say. *My friend had a premonition that you might be shot at some unknown time in some unknown location* probably isn't going to cut it."

"Yeah. I guess we do need more information. Let's see if we can find any current cases that Trinity and Bryson were working on together," I suggested.

Woody stood up. "I'm going to go into my office and make a few calls. I won't be long if the two of you don't mind waiting."

I glanced at Trevor. He shrugged.

"Okay," I said. "We can wait."

Woody picked up his sandwich and his soda and headed back toward his office.

"I'm really sorry about this," I said to Trevor. "Tracking down the person who shot a social worker in her driveway is not the relaxing getaway we talked about."

"It's not a problem at all," Trevor said. "If there is anything either of us can do to help Woody out, I think it is important to do so. It did occur to me that we might fit in some relaxation around helping Woody."

I leaned in just a bit. "Oh. What did you have in mind?"

"I have a new recipe I've been wanting to try out. If you don't mind being a guinea pig, I thought we could have dinner at my place."

"Well, I'm not sure how I feel about the guinea pig part, but I'm game. I'm sure whatever you make will be delicious. Are you still planning to take the weekend off?"

"I am since I'd already planned to be off, and it is a slow time of the year, I figured we'd do what we could to help Woody but maybe work in some fun as well. There is a pub that recently opened down the coast that I've been wanting to try out. If we have time, maybe we can take a drive."

"Sounds fun." I looked up when Woody returned to the room. "Well?"

"Based on the conversation I had with Bryson's assistant, he has three cases he is working on with Trinity. One case is a child custody case involving the maternal grandfather of seven-year-old twins and their stepdad. The biological mother named her husband as guardian of her daughters should anything happen to her, but apparently the woman's father, the grandfather of the twins, is suing for custody."

"And the biological father?" I asked.

"As far as I can tell, he is not now nor has he ever been in the picture, but I only received a brief summary and am waiting for more details about the case."

"Okay, what else are they working on?" I asked.

"Trinity was working on a neglect case involving four children aged ten and under who were left alone much of the time while the parents were working or otherwise occupied. Apparently, she has tried working with the parents to rectify the situation, but two weeks ago, the oldest was trying to cook dinner for his siblings and set fire to the kitchen. Trinity and Bryson worked together to have the children removed from the home. The father was arrested after he picked them up from school without permission with the intent of taking them to stay with his brother who lives in Utah. It's a pretty big mess."

"Sounds volatile enough to lead to someone going over the deep end. And the third one?" I asked.

"The third case involves a fifteen-year-old boy named Devon Long, who has been in the foster care system since he was four. Both of his parents were sent to prison for armed robbery. The boy's mother was released from prison early due to overcrowding and for good behavior. She has petitioned to have her son returned to her, but the foster parents are balking. When they accepted the child into their home for such a long-term assignment, they were concerned about becoming too attached, but they were told the boy's parents would be in prison until after he turned eighteen, so having him returned to either parent wouldn't be an issue."

"And now it is an issue."

"Exactly."

"So what is the plan at this point?" I asked.

"I'm going to speak to all three parties, and I plan to track Bryson down and speak to him personally. He is going to be in court until four, so I plan to catch up with him there."

Wadding up my sandwich wrapper, I tossed it in the trash. "Okay. It sounds as if you have that handled. I'm going to go by the hospital again tomorrow and try to connect with Trinity. I don't have high hopes that I will be able to, but I'm willing to try. In the meantime, if you need anything, call or text. I'll be around, but I may not be home, so just call my cell."

"I will, and thanks again. I'll let you know how my interviews with the three people of interest go. When it comes to child custody, there is always the potential for a peaceful negotiation to turn volatile."

I stood up to leave when an image flashed through my mind. "I had another image," I said aloud. "It was the same man I'd seen before being shot again, but this time I noticed the setting. He was standing on the stairs in front of the courthouse."

Woody frowned. "Maybe I'd better head over there now."

"Yeah. I think you should. This image was different than the last one. This one felt as if I was seeing it in real-time."

The woman who manned the front poked her head in through the door of the conference room where we were still talking. "There has been a shooting at the courthouse. A man is dead. All units in the area have been dispatched to respond."

Woody grabbed his vest and his gun. "I'm on my way."

Books by Kathi Daley
Come for the murder, stay for the romance

Zoe Donovan Cozy Mystery:
Halloween Hijinks
The Trouble With Turkeys
Christmas Crazy
Cupid's Curse
Big Bunny Bump-off
Beach Blanket Barbie
Maui Madness
Derby Divas
Haunted Hamlet
Turkeys, Tuxes, and Tabbies
Christmas Cozy
Alaskan Alliance
Matrimony Meltdown
Soul Surrender
Heavenly Honeymoon
Hopscotch Homicide
Ghostly Graveyard
Santa Sleuth
Shamrock Shenanigans
Kitten Kaboodle
Costume Catastrophe
Candy Cane Caper
Holiday Hangover
Easter Escapade
Camp Carter
Trick or Treason
Reindeer Roundup
Hippity Hoppity Homicide

Firework Fiasco
Henderson House
Holiday Hostage
Lunacy Lake
Celtic Christmas – *December 2019*

Zimmerman Academy The New Normal
Zimmerman Academy New Beginnings
Ashton Falls Cozy Cookbook

Tj Jensen Paradise Lake Mystery:
Pumpkins in Paradise
Snowmen in Paradise
Bikinis in Paradise
Christmas in Paradise
Puppies in Paradise
Halloween in Paradise
Treasure in Paradise
Fireworks in Paradise
Beaches in Paradise
Thanksgiving in Paradise

Whales and Tails Cozy Mystery:
Romeow and Juliet
The Mad Catter
Grimm's Furry Tail
Much Ado About Felines
Legend of Tabby Hollow
Cat of Christmas Past
A Tale of Two Tabbies
The Great Catsby
Count Catula
The Cat of Christmas Present

A Winter's Tail
The Taming of the Tabby
Frankencat
The Cat of Christmas Future
Farewell to Felines
A Whisker in Time
The Catsgiving Feast
A Whale of a Tail
The Catnap Before Christmas

Writers' Retreat Mystery:
First Case
Second Look
Third Strike
Fourth Victim
Fifth Night
Sixth Cabin
Seventh Chapter
Eighth Witness
Ninth Grave

Rescue Alaska Mystery:
Finding Justice
Finding Answers
Finding Courage
Finding Christmas
Finding Shelter – *Early 2020*

A Tess and Tilly Mystery:
The Christmas Letter
The Valentine Mystery
The Mother's Day Mishap
The Halloween House

The Thanksgiving Trip
The Saint Paddy's Promise
The Halloween Haunting
The Christmas Clause – *November 2019*

The Inn at Holiday Bay:
Boxes in the Basement
Letters in the Library
Message in the Mantel
Answers in the Attic
Haunting in the Hallway
Pilgrim in the Parlor
Note in the Nutcracker – *December 2019*

A Cat in the Attic Mystery:
The Curse of Hollister House
The Mystery before Christmas - *November 2019*

The Hathaway Sisters:
Harper
Harlow
Hayden – *Early 2020*

Haunting by the Sea:
Homecoming by the Sea
Secrets by the Sea
Missing by the Sea
Betrayal by the Sea
Thanksgiving by the Sea – *October 2019*

Sand and Sea Hawaiian Mystery:
Murder at Dolphin Bay

Murder at Sunrise Beach
Murder at the Witching Hour
Murder at Christmas
Murder at Turtle Cove
Murder at Water's Edge
Murder at Midnight
Murder at Pope Investigations

Seacliff High Mystery:
The Secret
The Curse
The Relic
The Conspiracy
The Grudge
The Shadow
The Haunting

Road to Christmas Romance:
Road to Christmas Past

USA Today best-selling author Kathi Daley lives in beautiful Lake Tahoe with her husband Ken. When she isn't writing, she likes spending time hiking the miles of desolate trails surrounding her home. She has authored more than a hundred books in eleven series, including Zoe Donovan Cozy Mysteries, Whales and Tails Island Mysteries, Tess and Tilly Cozy Mysteries, Sand and Sea Hawaiian Mysteries, Tj Jensen Paradise Lake Series, Inn at Holiday Bay Cozy Mysteries, Writers' Retreat Southern Seashore Mysteries, Rescue Alaska Paranormal Mysteries, Haunting by the Sea Paranormal Mysteries, Family Ties Mystery Romances, and Seacliff High Teen Mysteries. Find out more about her books at www.kathidaley.com

Stay up-to-date:
Newsletter, *The Daley Weekly* http://eepurl.com/NRPDf
Webpage – www.kathidaley.com
Facebook at Kathi Daley Books –
www.facebook.com/kathidaleybooks
Kathi Daley Books Group Page –
https://www.facebook.com/groups/569578823146850/
E-mail – kathidaley@kathidaley.com
Twitter at Kathi Daley@kathidaley –
https://twitter.com/kathidaley
Amazon Author Page –
https://www.amazon.com/author/kathidaley
BookBub – https://www.bookbub.com/authors/kathi-daley

Made in the
USA
Middletown, DE